BILLY WHISKER'S ADVENTURES

FRANCES TREGO MONTGOMERY

Billy Whiskers' Adventures

CHAPTER I

THE CHUMS RETURN TO THE LAND OF THE FREE AND THE BRAVE

Billy Whiskers, Stubby and Button sailed by the Goddess of Liberty and entered New York harbor after being in France ever since our troops entered the War. They had gone over on one of the troop ships and it just so happened that they returned on the same ship and with the same Captain and crew.

They were returning home covered with scars and wounds received while performing acts of bravery, but what cared they for scars and wounds so long as they had not lost an eye, ear or leg, and were feeling perfectly well and strong? To be sure, Billy had lost the tip of his tail when he was blown up by a bomb, but that did not matter.

You never saw three such happy animals as these were to be able once again to lay eyes on their beloved country, — the United States of America, that glorious country of the free and the brave.

"Gee, I feel so happy I could jump out of my skin!" exclaimed Billy with glowing eyes as the three stood on deck watching the familiar shores slip by them and the skyscraper buildings grow taller and taller and taller as they approached them.

"See!" said Billy. "We are about to dock. Now the next thing to settle is where we are going when we first land."

But the question was settled for them in a most unexpected way. For before Billy's remark could be answered, all three of them felt ropes being slipped around their necks, and heard the loud guffaws of three sturdy sailors as they pulled the ropes tighter, saying, "This is the time we caught you fellows off your guard!"

"We surely caught you slick as a whistle," remarked one of the sailors. "And now we have you, we are going to carry out the Captain's orders and look after you until he hears from France whether we are to take you back to your regiments when we return with more troops or keep you here."

"Return to France?" whined Stubby. "Just when we reach home safe and sound after braving all the terrors of submarines, sunken mines and dropping bombs? To be captured and sent back is really too much! I don't feel as if I would survive the disappointment, do you, Billy?"

"Not on your life will I go back!" replied Billy. "Not unless they take me over dead. For I shall fight to the last drop of my blood before I submit to being shipped back."

"And so will I," said Button. "I'll scratch their eyes out first. And from this day forward I shall begin to let my claws grow long and sharp for that very purpose. I'll see whether or not they take me back!"

"But they haven't started back yet, and 'There's many a slip twixt the cup and the lip.' We'll have two or three weeks to make a getaway before they sail as they have to coal the ship before even thinking of sailing. And if in that time we three can't put our heads together and think of some way to slip through their fingers, we are pretty stupid and deserve to be shipped back. Don't pull back or make any fuss," counseled Billy, "but just go along with the sailors and watch for a chance to escape. It may come any minute. And remember if any one of us sees a chance, he is to take it and not wait for the others. Just get free and then wait around until the rest of us get loose."

"Seems to me you have a good deal of baaing to do this morning, Mr. Billy," said the sailor who was holding the rope around Billy's neck as he stood watching the ship tie up at the dock.

"Guess he must be giving orders to his Chums," replied a second sailor who had Stubby in charge.

"Seems like it," said the one who held Button. "I expected them to fight like the very dickens, didn't you?"

"I surely did," answered the one who had spoken first. "But it is not too late for them to show fight yet, and I bet all that talking His Royal Highness, King Billy, has been doing has been orders to his Chums to fight later on. You just wait and see."

Just then the Captain appeared on deck and ordered the sailors to take the goat, dog and cat ashore and tie them in the warehouse on the dock until he could find some place to board them until he heard from France what to do with them.

"They are too valuable to leave just on the dock. They might get loose or be stolen. Feed and water them and when I go up to the city I will look for some trustworthy person to take care of them. By the way, don't one of you know some one ashore who could house and feed them until we hear?"

"Aye, aye, sir!" replied one of the sailors. "I have an uncle who lives close to the docks. He keeps a small, cheap boarding-house for sailors. He is a very kind-hearted man and fond of pets. I could take them there and I am sure he would give them the best of care for very little recompense."

"Just the thing! Just the place for them!" exclaimed the Captain. "You may take them over there as soon as the gangplank is out. And you two boys go with him. He might have trouble trying to manage all three alone. Here is money to pay for the animals and to buy your own dinners. Tell your Uncle I'll foot the bill before we sail and throw in an extra dollar or two if he turns them over to me in good shape when we call for them."

"Aye, aye, sir!" replied the sailor.

"Well, this beats all the good luck I ever heard of," said Billy, "for we can get away from that boarding-house as easily as a cat laps cream."

"You are right, we can, and have plenty of time too to lay our plans as to what we will do when we escape," agreed Button.

"It looks as if we would sleep on feathers and eat fowl," said Stubby.

The three sailors took the three Chums over to the chop-house, where they were given a hearty welcome by the sailor's uncle. He was so glad to have his nephew back from the War unhurt that he gladly took in the animals to please him. And I really think that had his nephew asked him to let the Chums sleep in his beds instead of in a shed in the back yard, he would have consented. As it was, Stubby and Button came near having fits from the amount of meat they ate as the Uncle had given them the scrapings from the plates, making a pile of beef and chop bones a foot high. He also gave Billy so many vegetables and so much juicy fruit that he had cramps all night.

In the morning there was still plenty of food left for their breakfast, but the Uncle insisted on giving them a fresh supply of food and water.

"He is a mighty fine old man," said Billy, "and I feel like a villain planning to run away from him, but we must or run the risk of being sent back to our regiments in France, and I for one am sick to death of war."

About ten o'clock in the morning the Uncle and the three sailors came into the yard to see how the animals were faring, and the sailors seemed pleased with the way they looked.

"Now we can tell the Captain when we return to the ship that we saw the animals just before we went to the boat and that they were safe and sound and in a good home where they will be well cared for until he hears what to do with them."

"I guess I'll leave the door of the shed open," said the Uncle. "It will make it more cheerful for them. And I think we had better take those ropes off their necks as they can't get out of the yard without going through the house or jumping the fence, and it is much too high for them to do that."

Little did those sailors and the old man know of the jumping powers of these three animals or he would never have had them untied. When the sailors and the old man had disappeared in the house, the three Chums walked around the yard looking for a loop-hole to crawl through, or for a weak board Billy might butt down. As for Button, all he had to do was to run up the fence and jump down on the other side. And did they but know it, Stubby could do the same stunt as he had watched the police dogs in Paris run up the side of an eight-foot fence, balance themselves on the top and leap down on the other side. As for Billy, when he was ready to go he could jump on top of an old packing box that stood beside the shed, and from that leap to the roof of the shed. From there he could spring into the alley. But what bothered them now was where they should go when they escaped. The city was very large and it stretched itself out along the banks of the Hudson River for miles and miles. They wanted to go in that direction, as 'way up north lived Nannie, Billy's little wife whom he was crazy to see after his long absence abroad. She was away up in Wisconsin on the dear old farm and it would take weeks and weeks to reach there if they traveled by foot all the way. But they expected to steal some rides as they always did when traveling. Stubby and Button had not a relative in the world they knew of, but they loved Nannie and all of Billy's family as if they were their very own blood relations. They had known them for years and years and had always been very kind to them, especially Nannie and Daisy, Billy's son's wife, while the Kids, Billy's twin grandchildren, were their delight.

The three Chums were lying perfectly still, each engrossed in his own thoughts and plans as how best to get out of the city when they were aroused by a loud meow over their heads. Looking up, they saw a big, striped cat sitting on the fence.

"Good-morning, friends and distinguished travelers!" said the cat. "I hope I am not disturbing you, but the cats and the dogs of the neighborhood — and there is a goodly number of them — appointed me the head of a committee to call upon you and welcome you to our shores."

As the cat had been talking, other cats had been appearing on top of the fence and now a line of them, all sizes, colors and descriptions, sat on the top of the fence winking down at the Chums, while through holes under the fence appeared dogs' heads, as evidently they were too large of body to crawl through the small holes.

"The canary you see in the cage hanging out of that upper window, and the parrot in the window of the next house sang and called out to us this morning that celebrated travelers from the War had just arrived from overseas and were shut in Grandpa Stubbs' back yard. Every one around here calls Mr. Stubbs grandpa because he is so kind to little children and to all animals. We are always glad to hear some things of the outside world, and when we heard that you were fresh from the war zone, we determined to make your acquaintance and invite you to speak and tell us of some of your adventures on the other side. I am president of the Dog and Cat Information Bureau, and we are holding a meeting to-night in a big, empty warehouse that has just been finished for the storage of ammunition. We have a very large membership—five hundred dogs and cats belonging. Having no newspaper, we meet to exchange the news of the day. If we did not, we would not know what was going on in the world outside our city. As it is, we are well posted for dogs and cats journey here from all over the world to speak at our meetings and to tell us what is happening in the countries from which they come. Now I hope all of you will favor us by speaking at our meeting to-night. It begins at twelve o'clock, and I will come and escort you to our place of meeting. We start rather late as it is easier for us to steal away from our homes unmolested at that hour than at any other. Many of our members are children's pets and can't get away until they are tucked in bed as they keep such close track of them."

Billy stood up and bowing to the line of cats on the fence and to the heads of the dogs under the fence, he began:

"Friends and countrymen, we thank you for your courtesy and kind invitation to speak before your club this evening. This we will be pleased to do provided we can escape our host and are not locked in the shed. But I think I can promise you we will be there for if we should be shut in the shed, my good strong head can butt down and make short work of a board or two that would give us access to the alley. Should we be tied, we can easily chew the rope in two. Consequently I think you may expect us at the appointed hour if some one will kindly show us the way to where your meeting is to be held."

Just then Mr. Stubbs opened the back door, and stepped into the yard.

"Bless my soul! I never saw so many dogs and cats in my life. I must be seeing things, for surely there can't be that many cats and dogs in this neighborhood." He rubbed his eyes to make sure he had seen a line of cats sitting on top of the fence and a line of dogs peeping under the fence. But when he looked again, there was not a single cat or dog to be seen. The only ones he could discover were Stubby and Button, both apparently asleep outside the shed door.

"Well, I declare that is the most peculiar thing that ever happened to me in my life! I distinctly saw dozens of cats and dogs and now I can't see one. Heigho! My old eyes must be playing tricks with me." And that was all he thought about it. He had come out to shut the Chums in the shed, but seeing them all three fast asleep, he decided to let them sleep on and not shut them in the shed that night.

CHAPTER II

THE NEW YORK DOG AND CAT CLUB

He really is an accommodating old fellow, isn't he," said Billy, "to leave us out all night? It will save him a broken shed door, though he will never know it."

"What time do you suppose it is?" asked Stubby.

"From the height of the moon I should say it must be about half past ten," answered Button.

"That will give us an hour and a half to think up what we are going to talk about at the club to-night. What are you going to tell them, Billy?" said Stubby.

"I really don't know. Guess I will wait for the inspiration of the moment."

"You better think up something extra exciting. Why not tell them about the time you were blown out of the trenches and lost a piece of your tail? Or, better yet, when you broke into the German headquarters and butted the great Hindenburg himself," advised Button.

"Very well, I will, as probably that would be as interesting as anything I could recount. What are you two fellows going to relate to them?"

"I think I shall tell them about our trip on the canal boat in France," replied Button.

"And I plan to describe to them the Dog Hospital and tell how it was blown up by the Germans," added Stubby.

"It is quite an idea," said Billy, "their having a club like this. It keeps them in touch with all that goes on throughout the whole country. I am quite anxious to see what it is like."

As the hands of the clock in the Ferry station pointed to twelve, they heard a loud meow and looking up they saw the big cat that had first appeared to them sitting on the fence.

"Well, friends, here I am! Are you ready to start?"

"All ready!" replied Billy.

"But how are you to get out?"

"We will show you," said Stubby, whereupon Billy hopped up on the packing box and from it onto the roof of the shed and then jumped down into the alley.

"Very cleverly done!" commended the cat, whose name, by the way, was Tiger because he was striped like one. "But what puzzles me is how your friends are to get out as the jump is too high for them."

"Too high for them, did you say? Nothing is too high for a dog that has done police duty in France. Listen! Did you not hear something hit the fence and then the scratch of nails on the boards? Well, that is my friend Stubby running up the side of the fence. From the sounds, evidently he did not get enough of a running start and fell back. But here he comes! See his head appearing over the top?"

In a second Stubby appeared, balancing himself on the ridge of the fence. The next moment he stood beside them. At the same time Button also ran down a post of the fence.

"Now we are all here, we'll have to hurry to allow for having to stop to hide when we see watchmen and strange dogs. Not knowing any of our members, you will have to be careful not to attack them, thinking they are enemies. I will give you the password. It is three short, sharp barks. On seeing another dog, all our members bark this password and if the dog they bark at does not reply in like manner, they know it is a stray dog. The cats all give three caterwauls in the same manner."

"Oh," exclaimed Button, "here comes a brute of a bulldog, whose mouth looks as if it were just watering for the back of a cat. Unless he gives the password quickly I shall take no chance but run up this tree. I am willing to tackle almost any dog but a bulldog."

"Bow! Wow! Wow!" barked the bulldog as he approached them.

"Bow! Wow! Wow!" replied Stubby, while Billy baaed, "Baa! Baa! Baa!" and Button meowed, "Mew! Mew! Mew!"

By this time the bulldog had come up to them and Tiger introduced them, telling the dog what distinguished friends he was meeting.

They found him most agreeable and that his looks really belied him, just as the appearance of many persons does. As they all trotted along toward the big warehouse down by the dock, Stubby and the bulldog ran side by side, while Billy and the two cats ran on ahead. Presently Stubby barked: "Oh, Billy! What do you think? Our new friend here says he is the full brother of Boozer, the bulldog that belonged to Captain Percy, and that he was in the Dog Hospital at the same time we were there, laid up with a broken leg."

"The world is small after all. To think we should meet over here just after seeing your brother in France!"

"Hiss!" warned Tiger. "No more talking until we are inside the building. We are approaching the warehouse now and we must not let the watchmen see us. The only way we can get in is through a window in the basement that has been left open by mistake. There is a broad plank running from the window down to the floor that the men use with their wheelbarrows to carry out the dirt. It makes it very handy to get out. We all could jump down, but few of our club members can jump up so high. None of us can jump like Stubby here."

"Bow-wow!" barked the bulldog in a low voice as a man with a lantern turned into the alley down which they all were running. "Hide quickly until he passes!"

As the man passed them, they heard him muttering to himself: "I never saw so many cats and dogs in my life as I have seen to-night in this alley. I did not know there were so many in the world! And when I get up to where I saw them they are all gone—disappeared—vamoosed. They must be the ghosts of the dead and gone dogs and cats that used to live in the warehouse."

Just then the bulldog, whose name was Buster, sneezed, which so startled the man that he ran as if he had been shot.

"Nice brave watchmen they have!" said Billy.

"Plague take my nose!" said Buster. "It is so short and stubby that all the dust gets into it and to save my life I can't help sneezing. And I always do it at the most inopportune moment."

Just then a whistle sounded, and Tiger said, "We must hurry! There goes the twelve o'clock whistle at the factory down the river. It is the signal for the night shift to come on."

The warehouse being near where they were, in about five minutes they found themselves entering the low window Buster had spoken about. When they looked inside, it was pitch dark and as if they were looking into a coal pit. But their eyes being such that they could see in the dark, they had no trouble in walking the plank and soon found themselves on the floor of the cellar. It looked a black square in shape and there was absolutely nothing in it, Tiger said. Still in the distance they could see black shapes moving about.

"What in the world is over in that corner?" asked Billy.

"Oh, they are only wharf rats," replied Tiger. "Shall we charge down on them just for fun?"

"Say we do! But I hate rats as I do poison," said Billy.

"So do I, but they are our natural enemies," answered Tiger.

"Ours too," from Stubby.

"You stand and watch the fun, while we rat haters kill a few," suggested Tiger.

"Very well!"

"When I say three, all of you run for the bunch and kill as many as you can," instructed Tiger.

For the next ten minutes you never in all your life heard such squealing, snarling and snipping of teeth as there was in that cellar. Two unusually big cats and two dogs all bound to kill rats were fighting these fierce wharf rats. But what made the battle such a bloody one was that wharf rats are braver than house rats and will fight to the death when attacked. Being large, and having long, sharp teeth, more often than not they get the better of ordinary cats and dogs that are sicked on them. In less than fifteen minutes hundreds of rats had been killed, for Buster was a noted rat killer. All he did was to open his jaws, grab a rat in the middle of its back, give his head a shake and the rat's back was broken. Then he tossed that rat aside and served another one likewise.

The rats had all disappeared or else were lying dead in heaps when Billy heard Stubby give a whine of pain, and turning to discover where he was, he saw him standing in the midst of a pile of dead rats with one nearly half as large as himself hanging to his throat under his jaw. The rat had hold of Stubby in such a way he could not shake him off, and all the time the rat was sucking his blood.

Billy saw him in a minute and with one bound he was beside Stubby and had ripped the rat open with his long, sharp horn, which made its mouth open and set Stubby free.

"Thank you, old fellow, for saving me! I was almost gone when you came with your timely assistance."

"I guess we have had enough fun with rats for one night," said Tiger, "and we better be getting on or we will be late for the opening exercises."

"I am a perfect mess!" said Stubby in disgust. "See how bloody I am."

"So am I," replied Tiger.

"I too," chimed in Button.

"I tell you what let's do," proposed Stubby. "It won't take five minutes. Let's run out and take a swim in the river. I can never appear before a strange audience with my coat looking like this."

"I'll go with you," replied Buster.

"I think," said Button, "I would prefer cleaning my coat by rolling in that nice clean bank of sand in the corner of the cellar to swimming in the river."

"I am with you on that proposition," said Tiger. "No water for me when I can get good, clean sand! After a roll I shall come out as clean and shining as if I had been sent to the cleaner and run through a vat of gasoline."

Stubby and Buster went to the river and were soon swimming around and having great sport in the water as it was nice and warm. But presently Stubby stopped short and stared ahead of him, and what do you think he saw but a whole drove of rats swimming out to a big sea-going vessel that lay at anchor in the harbor.

"Let's go ashore. I've seen all the rats I want to see for a coon's age. And you can't get me out of here too soon for they may attack us."

Soon Stubby and Buster, looking as clean as whistles, found Button and Tiger who also looked spick and span, and the four entered the clubroom, which was on one of the upper floors and as light as day for the light from four big electric street lamps came streaming in the window, lighting the room from corner to corner and making it asbright as if the lamps were in the room itself. And what a sight was there! Hundreds of dogs and cats were there sitting on benches arranged in a semicircle and graduated like the seats in a theater. For this room had been used as a lecture room to give instructions to sailors and soldiers before going overseas, and the benches and platform were just as they had left them.

On the platform, sitting upon their hind legs on chairs one could see every specie of dog from the Eskimo dog of the North to the tiny hairless dog of the tropics. There were big dogs, little dogs, middle-sized dogs, and cats of all sizes, colors and breeds. The snow-white Angora was there as well as the mangy alley cat. But all were on an equal at these meetings and there was no quarreling between aristocrat and the animal with no pedigree. All was harmony there. Could only the human race be as harmonious as these animals, the Brotherhood of Man would be established.

One after another the cats and dogs went on the platform and either told some funny episode that had happened to them or some tragedy that had occurred where they lived, or else they described the country from which they had come, and told how the natives lived.

CHAPTER III

AN EXCITING EVENING

The first dog called upon to lecture was an Eskimo dog with bright, snappy eyes, short, sharply pointed ears, strong legs and a bushy tail that gave him the appearance of a wolf, especially as his coat was just the color of that animal. And what more natural, as the Eskimo dog is the direct descendant of the timber wolf of the North? And though they may appear docile at times, still they always retain that half wild, ferocious look and manner.

He was a handsome, alert dog and spoke in quick, short sentences and to the point. He began by saying:

"I expect that none of you are familiar with the far North, where it is day six months of the year and night the other six. But though the sun does not shine, don't think for a moment that we live in pitch darkness, for the stars and the Northern Lights make our nights most beautiful. In fact, they are more beautiful and varied than our days. Instead of the blazing rays of the sun that blind one, we have the ever varied, many colored rays of the Aurora Borealis, shooting stars and electrical displays of all kinds that far surpass even your most elaborate Fourth of July celebrations.

"One moment the sky will be a sea-shell pink, with bars of vivid green, lavender and purple playing across it, while in the center will be a misty golden ball as if the sun was trying to shine through. The next instant all may be pitch darkness until this too is chased away by another electrical outburst. These go on constantly for the whole six months until they become so common an occurrence that the inhabitants pay no more attention to those magnificent displays than you do to your sun on a summer day.

"Picture to yourself this wonderful sky, against which huge icebergs are seen, taller than your tallest church steeple, and more beautiful to look upon with their lacelike frostwork than your most elaborately carved white marble cathedral. All of this is reflected in detail in the clear, cold, deep green waters of the Arctic Ocean, where the big walruses, whales and seals live, to say nothing of the clumsy white polar bears that sit idly on a cake of ice waiting for an unwary fish to swim by so he may catch it and make a breakfast on it.

"In round-topped, oven-like mounds made of ice and snow live our masters, the Eskimos. They live on whale oil, blubber, fish and the meat of the musk ox, bear and other animals that inhabit the far North. You dogs and cats who live so far from us in a country where there are noisy cities cannot imagine the silence of a cityless country or a land where the only sounds are the crunching of one iceberg against another or the roar and thunder of a glacier as it falls to pieces when melted by the sun. This world of ours seems like a dead world when compared to yours, but underneath this eternal covering of snow, down deep in the green water of the ocean are myriads of living, moving creatures as lively as any in your more sultry climate.

"But I see I am taking up too much time, so will stop and extend an invitation to one and all of you to come and visit my Land of the Midnight Sun, and see for yourselves how things look and how we live. I thank you for your courtesy in listening to my stupid speech," and bowing low his head he left the platform.

His speech was followed by loud barks and meows and a great scratching of claws upon the bare floor.

At last it was Billy's turn to go on the platform. He had just been introduced to the large audience and had started to speak in the old-fashioned way by saying, "Friends and fellow countrymen!" when there was a terrific explosion and the window panes were blown in or shattered, while through the open windows could be seen vivid red and yellow lights and columns of black smoke. Every heart in that large assembly stood still for a moment, then one and all started for the exit.

"Some one is trying to blow up the docks. We better get out of here before this building goes up in smoke," said Billy. "All stick together, though. If we do become separated, come to our back yard."

Bing! Bang! Bang! and the walls of the building they were in began to tumble around them and the floor crashed in, falling on those that were in the cellar. As it happened, our friends had not been near the exit, so were not among the first to get out. This probably saved their lives as it kept them from being among those in the cellar when the floor fell.

"I say we take our chance and jump from one of the windows," said Billy, "before the whole building falls in on us or it blows up."

It was a long way to the ground, but the cats and dogs jumped down on the heads of the crowd that had gathered, and this broke their fall. Being very large, Billy could not do this so he ran to another window and leaped down on a high pile of baled stuff which was nice and soft on which to alight.

When they were all safely on the ground they made for the back yard of the chop-house as fast as their legs would carry them. But somehow they became separated from the bulldog and Tiger, so lost their way and never again were they able to find the old uncle of the sailor.

They wandered around for the rest of the night looking for a place to sleep, but they were careful to keep close together so they would not lose each other.

About daylight they found themselves on the bank of the Hudson River opposite a dock where lay a big pleasure boat. No one was astir on it, so they cautiously crept on board, thinking to get a free ride up the river. This would give them a lift on their journey north. All three found good places to hide in different parts of the boat, and they lay down and fell asleep for they were both tired and sleepy after all the excitement they had been through.

Billy was awakened by the scrubbing of the decks over his head.

"I can't see why the captains of boats always insist on scrubbing decks so early in the morning. I guess it is just because they are afraid the sailors will get fat unless they keep them working from sun-up to sun-down. I smell bacon cooking, and I just love it, though I am a goat. I can't get to sleep now that I have once been wakened, so I think I will go and see if I cannot get some of it to eat."

Billy crept to the head of the stairs that led down into that part of the boat where the kitchen was located, but just as he was about to venture down, he saw a sailor coming up. He dodged out on deck, and ran toward the prow of the boat. Here he spied another flight of stairs going down into the boat he knew not where. But what cared he? He would go down and see. They led down into the dining saloon and at the further end he could see a swinging door through which came the smell of frying bacon.

"I know the kitchen must be behind those doors. I'll just stick my nose against one of them and peek in."

Billy was just about to push one of the doors open when bang! came one of them against his head with such force that it knocked him over. It also rebounded with such force that it knocked over a sailor who was carrying a tray of glass tumblers to set on the table. Over went the man, rolling over and over amidst the broken glass and rattling tin tray.

Of course all this racket brought the cook and all the other deck hands who heard it. The cook still carried the frying pan in his hand, being too much surprised to set it down when he heard the noise. The man with mop and pail who had been scrubbing the deck came and also two or three other deck hands. There they all stood, staring with open mouths and bulging eyes at Billy, who had risen to his forefeet and stood surveying the wreck he had made. He still felt a little dazed but came to his senses in a hurry when he saw the man with the pail and mop raise the mop to come after him. Before the fellow had takentwo steps, Billy had risen to his hind feet, gave a spring and butted him straight into his pail, where he stuck fast and could not get up without the pail sticking to him. Then Billy whirled and hooked the pan of bacon out of the cook's hands, which sent it flying out the open window onto the deck. Then he turned and started for the other two men who were standing there, but they had seen enough and disappeared while there was yet time. Seeing the coast was clear, Billy wheeled around and ran out on deck, where he saw Stubby and Button eating up the bacon that had spilled out of the frying pan as it went through the window.

"Leave me a slice of that bacon and then run, for we shall have to get off this boat in double quick time if we expect to save our bacon," said Billy, thinking the slang expression very fitting indeed.

"Why, what is up?" asked Stubby.

"Didn't you hear a racket going on in there?"

"No. We just came down from the upper deck."

"Well, take my word for it and vanish before you are hit with a club or thrown overboard. I'll be with you as soon as I lick up this grease. Since you have eaten all the bacon I had so much trouble to get, I am not going to lose this grease anyway."

Splash bang! came water, bucket and all down on Billy's head. Quick as lightning, Billy jumped through the window through which it had come, and found himself standing face to face with the cook, who had the most astonished expression on his face you ever saw when he beheld Billy coming through the high, small window.

Billy stood on his hind legs and knocked the jaunty little white cook's cap off the man's head with one of his fore legs before the cook could defend himself or turn to run. They were in very close quarters as a ship's kitchen is not the largest room in the world. At last the cook got up enough courage to strike out at Billy. He intended to hit the goat in the stomach as he stood towering before him, but alas! his knuckles hardly touched Billy's stomach when he found himself flying backwards across the long, narrow room, out through the opposite door and hit the railing of the boat so hard it broke and let him fall splash into the water.

On perceiving this, Billy turned and ran off the boat, and soon found Stubby and Button, who were waiting for him. When they had gotten far enough away for safety, they stopped under a large shade tree and had a good laugh at Billy's recital of how he butted the cook overboard.

"It will do him good," said Button. "I bet it will be the first bath he has had in weeks."

"Bet so too," agreed Stubby.

"Well, what are we going to do now?" asked Billy. "That bacon has made me more hungry than ever. The salt in it has just whetted my appetite."

"Mine too," said Stubby. "I feel as if I could drink the river dry, I am so thirsty."

"Say we trot along this drive that runs by the river until we come to some house that has a yard around it, where we can hide until we have a chance to sneak into the house or stable to see what we can find to eat," proposed Button.

They had to travel several miles to find such a place for they were still in the suburbs of New York City and not far enough out for the summer homes with their beautiful grounds. Once they passed a roadhouse where they got a drink out of a watering trough for animals and stole a few mouthfuls of food from some baskets a greengrocer had left outside the kitchen door. Button and Stubby stole only meat and went running off, Button with a big lamb chop between his teeth and Stubby with a huge steak, while Billy contented himself with a head of lettuce. They were just rounding a bend of the road when they heard an excited Frenchman calling to them. Turning to look, they saw the French cook wildly waving his arms at them and calling to them to bring back his things. But they only kicked up their heels at him and disappeared from his view around the bend in the road.

"Gee!" exclaimed Stubby, "this steak is the best thing I have had to eat in a fat goose's age."

"Yum! Yum!" replied Button. "It can't beat this chop for tenderness and juiciness."

"Nor my head lettuce. It is as sweet as sugar and as cold as ice. I just dote on cold, crisp lettuce. The colder and more crisp, the better. But I am afraid that cook will have an apoplectic fit if he isn't careful, the way he was waving his arms and carrying on. Excitement such as that is very bad for a fat old cook of forty."

"Hark! I hear an auto coming from the roadhouse. We better get back farther in the bushes and hide until it passes. They might be after us," said Stubby.

But they were not pursuers, but only two young fellows chatting and laughing over the dismay of the cook, for he had called to them that if they saw a big goat, small dog and black cat to run over them and kill them dead, dead, dead!

CHAPTER IV

AN UNEXPECTED SHOWER BATH

Just at dusk the next day Billy, Stubby and Button entered a small town to look for some nice quiet place for them to sleep, for they had traveled far that day and were tired of being chased by dogs and stoned by boys. So when they came to a small bungalow on the outskirts of the town with a cellar door open and no one around to drive them away, the three stepped in as noiselessly as possible and crept down the cellar stairs to find a place to hide until the family had gone to bed. Then they would begin to look about for something to eat for they expected to find potatoes and probably other vegetables there for Billy to eat and some kind of cold meat for Stubby and Button, and perhaps a pie or piece of cake, either of which would be very acceptable to all of them for they dearly loved sweets of all kinds.

The corners of the cellar were quite dark as by this time the sun had set, so Billy hid himself in one corner behind a pile of kindling, while Stubby crawled under the stationary wash tubs and Button curled himself up on top of a high pile of boxes, from which place he could see a swinging shelf with a plate of cold meat and boiled potatoes, as well as an uncut pie and some doughnuts on it. In the opposite corner of the cellar Billy spied a pile of potatoes and some cabbage and carrots.

"Well, I declare," exclaimed Button, "if we are not lucky! Here we find a good supper all laid out that will just suit our different tastes. Meat and potatoes for Stubby, as well as potatoes, cabbage and carrots for Billy."

"Hark! I hear some one coming!" warned Stubby. "I do hope whoever it is, they don't find us and drive us out just when a good supper is in sight, and also a nice quiet place to sleep."

Clumpety, clump, clumpety, clump, down the stairs came a stupid looking German girl with a plate of fried chicken in one hand and a dish of lovely crisp lettuce in the other. These she put on the shelf and then turned and stumped her way up the stairs again. Then they heard her locking up for the night, as they thought, but soon she appeared wearing her hat and went out the side door through which they had come into the cellar. They all kept very still for a little while, then Button meowed to Stubby to tell him what he could see on the shelf for them to eat, and where Billy could find some potatoes and other vegetables. Stubby crawled out from under the tubs and ran to where Button said the shelf was, but alas, alack! how was he to get at the things on the shelf? It was six feet above him and so hung from the ceiling that there was absolutely no way for him to climb up to it.

"Gee whiz! It makes me hungrier than ever to smell all those goodies and not be able to get at them!"

While Stubby was standing there trying to think out a way to reach them, Button cautiously climbed down from the boxes onto the shelf and with his nose and paw poked a big, round potato and a thick slice of meat off the plate to the floor. As they fell, they hit Stubby on the nose and made him jump, it was so unexpected, and at first he thought some one was throwing things at him. While he ate the meat, Button helped himself to fried chicken and Billy came over and baaed to him not to be so greedy but to throw him down some lettuce.

"Why don't you go over into that corner and eat those carrots and other vegetables?" meowed Button.

"Because I am not such a goose as to eat cold, dirty potatoes and cows' food when I can get my favorite nice, crisp lettuce."

The three ate and ate, for they were very hungry after their long tramp on the road all day. After Button had pushed all the food onto the floor he did not want for himself, and had licked the plate, he said, "I wish I had a nice drink of milk now, to quench my thirst. If I had that, I could go to sleep and sleep until daylight without waking, even if a rat chewed my tail and a mouse bit my ear."

"A pail of clean, cool water would please me better," said Billy.

"Me too," said Stubby. "Listen! I hear water running somewhere," he added.

"It sounds to me as if it were in the kitchen upstairs," said Billy. "I don't hear any one stirring around up there, so let us go and get a drink and then turn in for the night."

Billy walked to the cellar stairs and was half way up, while Stubby and Button were just behind him, when they heard some one exclaim, "Chester, come quick! Come quick! The water is running in the sink, and the cellar floor is flooded."

This was followed by the loud laughter of two people.

"Whatever shall we do?" said a girl's distressed voice.

"Get a mop and mop it up!" replied a boy.

"But the mop is in the cellar and I'll get my feet wet if I cross the floor to go to the cellar. Besides, I have on my best white shoes."

"Where do you keep the broom? That will do."

"Behind the kitchen door usually, but with the house all torn up with housecleaning, I don't know where it is."

"I'll find it. You stay out of the room so you won't get wet."

"Who ever would have thought that just because I happened to set that coffee pot over the hole in the sink that it would stop it up so tight that the water when it overflowed the coffee pot would fill the sink and make it overflow?"

"No one would," answered the boy. "And here is all this mess just because we hadn't any sense and tried to cool a bottle of ginger ale by setting it in the coffee pot and letting the water run on it."

The three listeners on the stairs heard the boy cross the kitchen and turn off the water. Then they heard him get the broom from behind the kitchen door.

"Where are you going to sweep the water?" asked the girl.

"Down the cellar stairs! It won't hurt anything down there," and before Billy, Stubby or Button could move, a deluge of water struck them full in the face, blinding them and sousing them from the tips of their noses to the ends of their tails.

This made Button sneeze, and he climbed back to the top of the boxes. Billy turned on the stairs, but before he could really face about, another sweep of the broom sent a second deluge on him, and blinded by water and mad with rage, he rushed up the stairs to escape it. Instead of getting out of the way, he ran straight into the boy who was sweeping, which surprised the boy so that he let go the broom handle and it too flew out of his hands and hit Billy on the head. This made Billy so angry that he jumped for the boy and butted him straight into the sink, where he sat down in the overflowing basin. The girl, too panic-stricken to move, stood in the doorway wringing her hands and crying, "Don't butt me, Mr. Billy Goat! I didn't do a thing!"

She looked so funny standing there wringing her hands and calling Billy Mr. Billy Goat that just for fun Billy thought he would give her a very little butt into the next room — not enough to hurt her, but just to frighten her a little. But when she saw him coming toward her, she screamed and ran. Billy pursued her into a bedroom, where he overtook her and gave her a gentle butt that landed her in the middle of a big four-poster bed, after which he turned and trotted off to see what the boy was doing. He found him floundering in the sink, trying to get out that he might go to the girl's rescue, but he could not as his feet would not reach the floor and he could get no grip on himself in the slippery sink. Just at this crisis the maid came home and unlocked the outside door at the head of the cellar stairs. With one bound Billy was at the door the minute it was opened. As he flew by her, he hit her, knocking her over against the young man who was seeing her home. He held a watermelon under his arm, on which they intended to feast, but when Billy struck the girl and she fell against him, it sent the watermelon flying from under his arm and the three of them, Billy, the maid and her beau, all fell on the melon. This squashed it flatter than a pancake and made it explode like a bomb. While all this was taking place, Stubby and Button made their escape through the open door and ran down the street to wait for Billy to join them.

When he came up, all he said was, "Just our luck, to have to lose a perfectly good lodging place just when we were almost ready to go to sleep for the night! And just because two young geese could not drink ginger ale warm instead of cold!"

"But I would not complain if I were you, Billy," said Button, "for we got a good supper before it happened."

"Sure enough! So we did. I guess I better not complain. One thing, it is a nice warm night, so it wouldn't be bad to sleep outdoors, and I see a clump of trees and bushes down by the lake. Let's go down there and see if we can't find a nice soft mossy bank to sleep on."

So the three trotted off and soon found a soft sandy bank under some sheltering trees and bushes where they curled themselves up and were soon fast asleep.

CHAPTER V

WHAT HAPPENED ON THE FOURTH OF JULY

They were awakened at daybreak the next morning by a battered tin falling on their heads, followed by a shower of pieces of red paper.

All three jumped up and were wide awake in a second for all around them was the din of battle. For a moment they thought they were back in France and that a big bombardment was on. But on looking through the trees under which they had been sleeping, they saw a crowd of boys shooting off firecrackers and putting bunches of them under barrels and tin pans.

"This is no place for us!" exclaimed Billy. "I despise the Fourth of July and its celebration, and this is just what it is. If those boys see us, it will be all up with us, for if there is one thing boys love, it is to torture animals on the Fourth by tying bunches of firecrackers and tin cans on their tails."

"Well, thank goodness, my tail is so short they will have a good time tying anything on it," exulted Stubby.

"Mine too!" replied Billy.

"But how about mine?" said Button. "It is long enough to tie a whole string of crackers to it."

While they were talking, the boys started to run in their direction and came straight toward them. When they were within hearing distance, the Chums heard them say, "Let's pretend the trees and bushes are a fort. We'll put a lot of powder around them and blow them up."

"What did I tell you?" said Billy. "There is no safe place for men or beasts on the Fourth of July if there is a boy within a hundred miles."

"What shall we do?" asked Stubby. "If we stay here we will be blown up or maimed for life. And if we run out, the whole pack will probably set upon us."

"I say we show fight anyway," said Button. "In the first place, they don't know we are here and in the second we have the advantage of taking them by surprise. Billy, you can butt them while Stubby bites their heels and I will run up their backs and scratch the shirts off their shoulders."

"Good idea, Button!" commended Billy. "You should have been a General, at least, in the army."

"Oh, stop your fooling and mind when I hiss we all jump out of the bushes at once and attack our victims. Select the boy you will attack as they come toward us."

"All right," replied Billy. "I'll attack that big, red-headed boy who seems to be the leader."

"And I'll go for that snub-nosed, freckled-faced urchin with the ragged pants, as he seems to be displaying a fine amount of shins at present," said Stubby.

"Then I'll go for that boy who runs with his head and shoulders down. It gives me a good expanse of back to scratch," said Button.

On came the boys, whooping and hallooing with all the power of their lungs. But when they were within twenty feet of the trees and bushes that concealed our Chums, they jumped out at them. The leader stopped in his tracks, too dazed and surprised to move at seeing a strange goat come flying out of the bushes straight toward him with head lowered to butt. He scarcely had time to know he was surprised when he was hit in the pit of the stomach and sent sprawling in the sand fifteen feet away. As he picked himself up he saw a funny sight—a big boy running straight for the lake with a big, black cat sitting on his shoulders scratching the shirt off his back. Button never moved, but stuck to him as the boy swam farther and farther out. At last it seemed to occur to the boy to dive, which he did and Button, hating the water as all cats do, jumped for a big rock that was sticking out of the water. There he sat and meowed for Billy to swim out and carry him to shore on his back as he had often done before. But Billy was nowhere in sight. After butting the boy he had disappeared as completely as if the earth had opened and swallowed him.

As for Stubby, he had chased all the boys up town, first biting one boy's shins and then attacking another until he had driven them howling two or three blocks from where they started. When he saw he had gotten the boys so far away, he stopped chasing them and went back to see what Billy and Button were doing. But when he reached the old spot neither Billy nor Button was anywhere in sight. All he could see was a black object on a rock sticking out of the water. It looked like some one's wet muff or old coat. He did not know that that same wet muff was his own beloved Button.

Button was meowing as loudly as he could for Stubby to swim out and rescue him, but the wind was in the wrong direction to carry his voice to Stubby. Stubby looked around and even set up a howl, trying to find out where Billy and Button had gone, but no answering call came back. He sniffed around but could get no scent of them. Then all of a sudden he saw a boy come out of the lake and run up the shore. He started after him on a dead run, thinking that perhaps he would lead him to some boys who might have captured Billy. He was running with his head down when all of a sudden he pitched headlong into a dry well. What was his surprise on opening his eyes after the shock to find himself staring into Billy Whiskers' eyes!

"How in green gooseberries did you get here?" he asked.

"Same way you did! I took a header and here I am! I have baaed my head nearly off calling to you and Button to come to my rescue, but not a sound could I hear. Somehow or other my voice did not seem to carry."

"We certainly are in a pretty pickle! Lost in an abandoned well on a lake shore with no habitation within a quarter of a mile. This will be our tomb unless some one chances to pass this way soon. And the chances are that no one will pass this way for weeks."

"Where can that cat be?" asked Billy. "It sounds to me as if he too was in a hole or shut up somewhere and cannot get out."

"Yes, where can he be?" echoed Stubby. "First we hear his voice, then we don't hear it. It sounds a good way off at that. Say, Billy, I think I see a way out. You stand up on your hind legs and I will run up your back and see if I can't jump out of this well. It isn't more than eight feet deep and when you stand up you must be about six or seven feet tall."

"Yes, I should think I would measure that. But how are you to get room to get a running start?"

"I can't do that. I shall just have to climb up your leg by pulling myself, holding onto your hair and digging my claws into your back."

"Thanks! That sounds fine for me, I am sure!"

"Well, isn't it better than staying here and saving your skin and dying of hunger and thirst?"

"I suppose it is, but when you are out, how do you propose getting me out, as there will be no one up whose back I can run and jump?"

"Oh, that will be all right! When I am out, I can run and bring some one to help you out."

"Yes, I know, Mr. Stubby-tail. But do you realize that it is going to be some job to get a goat of my size out of a deep, narrow hole like this?"

"To be sure I do! But that can easily be accomplished when once I find a man to accompany me here to see what is down in this well. Men with pulleys can soon hoist you out."

"Well, I hope so, for I am getting tired already of being confined here. Just hear that cat howl now!"

"Listen! I hear voices. He must see some one walking on the beach. I hear two people talking and they are coming this way! Let's baa and bark for all we are worth!"

This they did, and a little girl and her father who were walking along the beach heard the meow of a cat come floating to them across the water and the baa of a goat and the bark of a dog float to them from the land on the other side. Still they could see no cat, dog or goat. All they could discover was a black coat or something like it lying out on the rocks.

Presently the little girl cried out, "Oh, papa, see! The coat is moving! It isn't a coat at all, but a cat. Did you see its long tail?"

"Sure enough, it is a cat. Most likely some bad boy has thrown it in the water with a stone tied to its neck, to try to drown it, but it has managed to crawl up on the rocks."

"Poor kitty! Let us go get our rowboat and bring it off. Will you, papa?"

"Yes, dear; if you want to, we will."

On their way to get the boat they passed within a few feet of the well, and though they heard both Billy's and Stubby's voices they could see them nowhere, and the wind played sad havoc for it made their voices sound as if they came from the opposite direction. After stopping several times and listening without being able to decide where the animals were, they walked on. Billy and Stubby could hear their voices die away in the distance.

"Now, Billy, there is a chance lost, so stand up and let me see if I can't climb up on your back and get out."

It took many trials, but at last by Billy putting his hind legs against one wall of the well and bracing his forehead against the opposite wall, Stubby managed to jump on his back and climb to his head, from where he gave a big leap and landed outside the well.

"Now, Billy, don't worry! I will soon find some one to get you out. If I don't, I promise you on my sacred word of honor to come back here and die with you."

It was not a rash promise on Stubby's part for already he had seen the man and his little daughter rowing out to take Button off the rocks.

"Now is my chance," thought he. "Here is a kind-hearted man going to the rescue of a cat. Why won't he be a good one to come to the aid of a goat? I'll go down by the shore and wait until they land. Then I will bark and run up to the well and make such a fuss that they will follow me to see what is down there."

Button was sitting on the little girl's lap enjoying the petting she was giving him when he saw Stubby standing on the beach, and he meowed to him, saying, "Well, old Chum, where have you been? And why didn't you come to help me off the rocks?"

To which Stubby replied, "Good reason enough! I fell into a well and only just now got out. And when you land you must help me make this man go to Billy's rescue."

"Why Billy's rescue? Where is he?" asked Button excitedly.

"Down the well, silly!"

"You said nothing about Billy being down a well, but only mentioned yourself. How in the world did you both happen to fall down a well?"

"Don't ask so many questions. Just do as I tell you to do now and after Billy is out I will answer all you wish to ask."

"Papa, this dog and cat must know each other. Just hear how they meow and bark messages to one another. He is a cute looking little dog, but this cat is a real beauty. He has such big yellow eyes just like glass buttons and his fur is so soft and silky. May I keep him for my very own?"

"Yes, dear, if you want to, for he does not seem to be wanted by anybody."

The boat had no sooner touched the shore than Stubby began making friends with the man and his daughter by walking on his hind legs, turning somersaults and doing all sorts of cute tricks. After he had done all his show tricks he ran over to where Billy was imprisoned, and ran round and round the rim of the well, looking in and barking very loudly. Then he ran back to the man and little girl and taking hold of the man's trousers leg he began to pull him in the direction of the well.

"What is the matter with you, you crazy little dog?"

Then Stubby let go his hold and raced back to the well. When he reached there, he jumped in, hoping this would bring the man and his daughter to the brink of the well to see what had become of him, and in trying to find out they would discover Billy.

His plan worked, for he had no sooner disappeared down the well than Button jumped out of the little girl's arms and ran after Stubby. The moment he saw Billy and Stubby both down at the bottom of the well, he too jumped in.

"I declare to goodness there must be some kind of a hole there, Nellie, and those animals have found something in it to interest them. We must hurry over and see what it is."

Can't you picture the surprise on their faces when they looked down the well and discovered a big Billy goat as well as the dog and cat they had followed?

"Bless my soul, Nellie, if there isn't a big, live goat down there! So we did hear a goat baa when we thought we did! Poor animal! I wonder if he was hurt when he fell in, for that is a nasty, deep hole. But the question now is how in the world are we going to get him out?"

"Yes, that is it," baaed Billy, but of course the man did not understand what Billy was saying to him.

"Poor thing! He may have been here for days and be nearly dead for want of food and water. But I guess not as he looks too fat for that. Nellie, run home and tell Tom to bring a pulley, rope and ladder from over on the lake where Mr. Stilwell's house used to stand before it burned."

Nellie was soon back from her errand, bringing her big brother and the hired man with her.

As Nellie's father turned his back to the well, Billy stood on his hind feet and Stubby climbed out of the well as he had once before. When Mr. Noland turned around, there was Stubby frisking around his feet.

"I'll be switched if here isn't that clever little dog again! How in the world do you suppose he got out of that well unless spooks boosted him?"

"Or the goat butted him out. That is more likely," replied his son.

"Now put the ladder down the well, and I'll go down and fasten the rope around the goat's body while you and Dan fix a brace to put the pulley on to pull him up," said Mr. Noland, ignoring his son's remark.

The hired man lowered the ladder into the well, but it had scarcely touched the bottom and found a secure footing when Billy climbed up the rungs as nimbly as a cat. This act made Mr. Noland's eyes fairly pop out of his head, while all the rest stood with open mouths. None of them had ever seen any animal as large as Billy climb a ladder. You see Billy's old circus stunts stood him in good stead once in a while. When he traveled with the circus, the clowns had taught him to climb a ladder halfway to the top of the big circus tent.

"I claim this goat as my own," said Nellie's brother.

"And I the cat!" said Nellie quickly.

"But where do I come in?" said their father. Just then Stubby barked, and Mr. Noland said, "Well, I'll take the dog and I think I have the best of the bargain at that, for he can almost talk. If it had not been for the dog, neither of you would have had a pet. It was he that led us to this abandoned well."

"You forget, father, that the cat showed you the way too," said Nellie.

"I think the best thing we can do now is to go home and get some supper and also give our new-found friends some food. I'll wager that they are hungry. They must have come a long way, for I never saw any of them around here before, and I know every dog and cat in the town. I won't say goat, for no one owns a goat," said Nellie's father.

So it happened that the Chums were given a good supper and beds of straw in the woodshed and then left to themselves for the night. At least that is what all of them thought, but the day being the Fourth of July made a difference for just as they were dropping off to sleep the stick of a Roman candle fell on the woodshed and burned a hole through the roof. Some sparks fell down and set fire to the straw on which the Chums were sleeping and in a few minutes straw, woodshed and all were in a blaze, and they only escaped with their lives because they were high jumpers and thus able to escape through the little window in the side of the shed. Billy was so large that he could not make it the first time, and he fell back into the fire, but the second time he went through, taking half the side of the woodshed with him. His hair was all on fire, but he had sense enough to roll in the sand and put it out instead of running. If you run when your clothes are on fire, you only feed the flames breeze you make and the fire burns faster than ever. When it was all out, Billy went down to the lake and had a good swim to rid himself of the smell of burnt hair.

When he came back, he was surprised to see a ring of people en-circling something that was making them laugh and clap their hands with delight. When he was near enough to stick his head between the crowd of people, what do you suppose he saw? There were Stubby and Button flying round and round, being chased by Fourth of July nigger chasers or snakes, as some people call this kind of fireworks. They are funny looking things that when set on fire twist and turn like live snakes, and no one can tell where they are going next. The consequences are that they are always surprising one and coming after them when they least expect it. The crowd had conceived the idea of making a circle so Stubby and Button could not run away, and then setting off a lot of these to chase them. It was Stubby's and Button's frantic efforts to escape that had caused all the fun and laughter.

"Here is the goat!" called out a lad. "Let's get him in the ring too!"

But instead of getting him in the ring as proposed, that lad found himself going up in the air like a balloon, one of Billy's mighty butts having sent him.

This broke up the party and when all had disappeared and the three friends were alone again, Billy said, "Didn't Itell you the Fourth of July was a bad day for animals?"

CHAPTER VI

BILLY WHISKERS MAKES TROUBLE AT SCHOOL

The next morning Mr. Noland took Stubby away out into the country with him in his auto, and Nellie carried Button over to her friend's to show her the big, fine cat she had found out on the rocks. Consequently Billy was left alone to amuse himself as best he could.

He wandered around for a while and at last went down to the lake and took a swim, coming out as clean and white as a fresh bale of cotton. Then not knowing what to do with himself, he decided to go up into the town and see how it looked to him. Not being a very large town, he had no difficulty in locating the main street and then the largest church, the movie theater and the schoolhouse. As he walked down the street, he stopped to help himself to a peach here and a plum there at the different fruit stands, as well as to several bunches of asparagus and a peck or two of green peas that he saw in baskets outside the grocery stores.

When he reached the schoolhouse he found it was recess time and all the children were out in the yard playing tag, leap frog, crack-the-whip and such games as children always play at school. Billy stood watching them for some time and as they seemed to be having such great fun, he thought he would go in and join in a game of pussy-wants-a-corner he saw four or five girls and boys playing. Much to the surprise of this group, the first thing they knew a big, white goat was running from tree to tree to get an empty corner just as they were doing. At first they were so astonished that they stopped playing, but soon they went on as Billy kept running from tree to tree, frisking his little paint brush of a tail and kicking up his legs with glee. You remember he had lost part of his tail in France in the war where it was blown off by a bomb which had sent him flying up in the air.

Presently all the children had stopped their games to watch Billy play pussy-wants-a-corner. He was just beginning to grow tired of the sport when the school bell pealed out that recess was over and all the children ran to form in line to march back to their rooms. Each room had a separate line of its own. When Billy saw this, he too went and stood in line. As he knew nothing about the different rooms, he selected a line in which stood a pretty little girl with yellow hair hanging in long braids down her back. She was the last one in the line, and being very busy talking to the little girl just in front of her, she did not notice that any one was standing behind her.

Billy overtook her and gave her a gentle butt that landed her in the middle of the bed.

"Her hair looks just like straw. It is just the color of it," thought Billy. "I wonder if it tastes like it too." And thereupon he began to chew the end of one of her braids.

"Stop pulling my hair, Jimmy Jones!" she cried, without turning around. Jimmy Jones and Tommy Green were in the habit of pulling her hair or giving it a twitch whenever they passed her. So now she took it for granted it was one of them when Billy pulled it while chewing on it.

"Didn't I tell you to stop pulling my hair? I'll tell teacher if you don't stop this minute!"

Billy did try to stop, but somehow her hair got between his teeth and he could not let go, much as he wished to do so. Of course the more he tried the worse it pulled. She turned quickly to slap the tease who was hurting her. But horror of horrors! She found herself face to face with the big goat that had been playing with them in the yard. She was terribly afraid of goats, and had stopped playing when Billy entered the game and had sat down on the school steps to watch them, so now she screamed as if she was being killed. This brought a teacher and some of the big boys to the rescue. By this time Billy was really pulling very hard in his frantic efforts to get loose, but he was unconscious that he was doing so. The little girl stood facing him, which wound her braid around her head and made it pull more than ever. Then too if she had only stood still, but she kept jumping up and down and calling out, "Take the nasty old goat away!"

When the teacher arrived, she soon saw what the trouble was and with the help of some boys she quickly removed the strand of hair from Billy's teeth, which released the little girl, who fell half fainting and crying in the teacher's arms.

On being freed, Billy trotted out of the schoolyard mumbling to himself that he would never try to eat hair again, even if it did look like straw. He was just about to run out of the school yard when he saw a boy enter eating a big red apple, with another still larger and more luscious looking in his hand.

"My, but those apples look good! I must have one, no matter what happens," thought Billy.

On seeing Billy coming toward him, the boy ran for dear life, trying to make the school door before Billy could overtake him. He did, but that was all. Billy had gotten a good whiff of the apples, and that settled it. He would have one of those apples, even if he had to chase the boy all over the school. He was hoping the boy would be so afraid of him that he would throw one of the apples at him. But no such good luck. Up the stairs ran the boy, trying to reach the room before Billy could catch him. Close on his heels came Billy. The boy dodged into his room and tried to shut the door but Billy was too close on his heels. So he ran around to the far side of the room, thinking surely the goat would not follow him there. But on came Billy more determined than ever to have one of those apples. Round the room they chased each other, with all the scholars standing up in their seats screaming and laughing and hugely enjoying the chase. By this time the boy was so afraid that his hair was standing straight up on end, and he was crying lustily. Had he known it was the apples that the goat wanted, he would gladly have given up both. He thought, of course, it was himself Billy wanted to butt. Now the extra large apple had been for his beloved teacher, and the second time around the room as the boy reached the platform where she stood, he made a dive for her and threw his arms around her waist, calling to her to save him, save him!

The teacher picked up a bottle of ink, the only thing on the table she could see to throw at Billy. It hit him on one horn and broke, and the ink began to run down into his eyes. This made Billy angry, so instead of chasing the boy, he decided to go for the teacher, butt her, grab the coveted apple from the boy and make his escape. Up on the platform he leaped, upsetting chairs as he went and overturning the table behind which the teacher and the boy had taken refuge. Billy shook the ink out of his eyes, leaped over the table and chairs, grabbed the apple out of the boy's hand, brushed against the teacher so hard that he knocked her over, stepped on her and then left the room.

On the way he ran into the principal of the school who had heard all the commotion and was coming to see what was causing it. Billy, never slackening his speed, ran straight into him, and landed the principal on his back, and as his head touched the floor his wig fell off. This mortified him so he let Billy go, and thought no more about him. All his effort was to get his wig on straight before any of the young lady teachers should see him. For he was very vain and he did not wish any of them to know he wore a wig. But alas! The more he tried to straighten it, the more it persisted in turning inside out and back end foremost. And there he sat with his bald head shining like a billiard ball when a sweet voice said, "I hope you are not hurt, Mr. Wheeler!" and looking up he saw standing before him the prettiest teacher in the whole school, the one above all others he would not have had see him in such a predicament for a whole year's salary.

"Oh, no, not at all, thank you!" he replied, as his nervous fingers tried to adjust his wig. He jumped to his feet and walked off as quickly as he could, trusting his wig was on straight. But when he reached his office and looked in the mirror, he found it was on hind side before, and the part at the back of his head when it should have been on top. From that day the boys nicknamed him Baldpate, though they took very good care that he never heard them call him that.

As for Billy, he found his delicious looking apple had a false heart and was worm eaten, so he had had all his trouble for nothing and gotten a nasty spot of black ink on his snow-white whiskers and hair.

"I guess I'll go back to Mr. Noland's and see if Stubby and Button have returned," he thought, and as he rounded the corner of the street on which Mr. Noland's house stood, he saw the auto turn in the other end of the very short block. Stubby jumped out and when he saw Billy he ran joyously to meet him, barking as he came, "Oh, Billy, you should have been with us! I never had more fun in my life. But what has happened to you? I bet you have been in mischief somewhere.

"Come down by the lake while I try to wash this ink off, and I will tell you what I have been up to while you were away, and you may tell me what has happened to you."

So the two of them trotted off toward the lake to recount their adventures. And as you are interested in the doings of Billy, Stubby and Button, perhaps you might like me to relate to you in another chapter what happened to each of them.

CHAPTER VII

BUTTON'S DAY WITH BELLA

Nellie took Button up in her arms and started over to see her best friend, Kittie Mead. Kittie owned a beautiful white Angora cat named Bella, who always wore a tiny gold bell tied around her neck with a blue ribbon.

When Nellie was within calling distance of Kittie's house, she began to call, "Oh, Kittie, bring your doll carriage here quick! Hurry, hurry, for this cat is getting heavy!"

Nellie had carried Button in her arms most of the way, as she was afraid that he would run away if she trusted him to follow her. Now Button was no lightweight, you must remember, and the farther she carried him, the heavier he became and the more he slipped through her arms. So when she called to Kittie most of Button's long body was dangling around her legs, while she still held on to his neck in such a manner that the poor cat was nearly strangled.

"Oh, Kittie, don't you hear me? Come, come, come! I can't carry this cat another minute!"

Luckily for Button, Kittie happened to be playing in the front yard with her doll and had just put Annabella, her favorite doll, to sleep in the doll carriage. So when she heard Nellie calling her, she jerked the sleeping Annabella out of the carriage so quickly it nearly disjointed her and tossed her on the grass while she started on a dead run down the garden path to meet the calling Nellie.

When Kittie came up, Nellie let go of Button and he dropped to the ground and lay like dead for a few minutes. Indeed, the poor cat was almost choked to death. Before he could recover and jump up and shake himself together enough to run away, Nellie had picked him up again and plumped him down in the doll carriage and the two girls began to talk as they wheeled the carriage toward the house. Nellie was relating to Kittie all that had happened since she saw her last, including the coming to her house of the goat, dog and cat, while Kittie talked so fast Nellie could not answer one question before she had asked two or three more. But neither of them noticed as all they wished was to talk, not to listen, anyway.

Button found the soft pillow in the doll carriage very comfortable and the motion made him sleepy, so he curled himself up a little tighter and went sound asleep. Had he known what they were planning to do, he never would have risked that, but would have jumped out and ran away. For these two little girls were planning to dress him up in doll clothes and play baby with him! Now that was one thing the dignified, independent Button could not stand. He had been used to play baby when a young cat, and he hated it. He had also made a vow that the very next person who tried to dress him up in doll clothes or any other clothes would be scratched for their pains.

All the way up the garden path the two girls discussed how they would dress him as well as what they would put on Bella. Button had been so sound asleep he had not heard a word. When the children left him asleep in the carriage to go after the clothes, he awoke and looking around spied a beautiful big cat with gray eyes looking down at him from the limb of a tree directly over his head.

"How do you do, Miss Beauty?" meowed Button when he had both eyes open and his thoughts collected enough to speak.

"I am pretty well. How are you, Mr. Impertinence?" Bella meowed back, for as you have guessed, this beautiful cat was none other than Kittie's pet, the belle of all the cats in that neighborhood, Miss Bella Angora Mead, to give you her full name.

"Come down and rest on this soft cushion beside me where we can talk without my having to crane my neck to look at you," Button invited.

"No, I can't. You better come up here unless you want to be tortured by being buttoned into a pink gingham doll dress and having a bonnet tied on your head. I heard the girls talking over what they were going to do to you and me, so I ran up here where they could not get at me. They will never think to look up here but will hunt all over the barn and wood piles for us, and perhaps even go down cellar, but look up a tree they never will."

"If that is what is about to happen, I surely will join you, as I object to being dressed up and having my fur turned the wrong way and having my ribs crushed by being buttoned into a tight dress."

"Well, if you are coming, hurry along for I hear them in the hall now and in another minute it will be too late for you to get up in the tree without them seeing you."

Button had barely climbed up in the tree and nicely settled beside Bella when the girls came running out of the house with their arms full of doll clothes. They went straight to the doll carriage, expecting of course to find Button asleep there.

"Oh!" exclaimed Nellie when she reached the carriage and found no Button. "He has run away!"

"He can't have gone far," replied Kittie. "Let's look for him. Perhaps he saw Bella and is getting acquainted with her. I'll call her and see."

So the two little girls began to call, "Bella, Bella! Sweetheart, where are you? Come here! Bella, Bella! Kittie, kittie, kittie!" as they walked around the yard and then behind the house looking under every bush and shrub. And all this time the two cats sat and grinned at them and enjoyed their discomfort very much.

After looking for the cats everywhere, the girls came back to thee front of the house and sat down by the empty doll carriage, scolding and telling each other what they would do when they laid hands on those two cats again. Presently one of the little girls threw herself back on the grass, her head on her hands, too angry to talk more. Lo and behold! What did she see but those two cats she had been talking about sitting quietly side by side on a limb over her head looking down on her. Yes, and from the expression on their faces she knew they were laughing at her!

"Nellie, Nellie, look up in the tree over your head and see what you will see!"

"Oh, you naughty, miserable cats! Come right straight down out of that tree this minute!"

"Oh, yes, we will be right down when we get good and ready," meowed Button.

"We are very comfortable up here, so you two better play with your dolls as we intend to spend the rest of the day up here," meowed Bella.

"You miserable cats, you! If I had hold of you, I'd pull your tails, so I would!" called Nellie.

"Better wait until you do get hold of us before you tell what you will do to us," meowed back Button.

"Let us throw green apples up at them and make them come down," suggested Kittie.

"All right. Let's do!"

"They make me laugh," said Button. "Neither one of them could hit the side of a barn even if they aimed at it. To try to hit us up here is perfectly ridiculous."

"I bet they hit themselves," meowed Bella. "Here they come with their aprons full of apples."

The girls began to throw the apples up in the tree but they could not even throw high enough to hit the limb on which the cats sat. And presently an apple came down and hit Kittie on the head.

"There! Didn't I tell you they would hit themselves?" said Bella.

Just then Nellie let out a cry and the cats laughed so they nearly fell off the limb for Kittie in her endeavor to throw high enough had whirled half way around and as she turned the apple flew out of her hand before she was ready and it hit Nellie squarely in the back.

"Let's not try to hit them any more," proposed Nellie wisely.

"I know what we can do. We'll go to the orchard and get the long ladder they are using to pick the cherries, and we'll put it up against the tree and then climb up after them."

"All right. Let's do!" again agreed Nellie.

Away ran the girls to the orchard and in about ten minutes the cats saw them tugging away at a long ladder. At last they reached the tree and after many mishaps succeeded in standing it up against the trunk. But what was their disappointment to find that it only reached half way up the tall tree and came nowhere near the limb on which the cats sat.

"I have it!" cried Nellie. "Let's get the hose and turn it on them. That will bring them down in a jiffy!"

Off ran the girls once again, the hose was brought and adjusted and the water turned on. But another disappointment awaited them. The force was not sufficient to throw the water far enough to reach the cats.

"Drat those cats!" exclaimed Kittie. "I am getting so mad I just must lay hands on them or explode!"

"I guess you will have to blow up then, or fly up to reach them," said Nellie. "The saucy things! Just see how they sit there and purr with contentment! Yes, I know they are laughing at us all the time!"

"I have it!" called out Kittie. "Give me the hose. I'll carry it up the ladder as far as it will reach and then I know it will be long enough for the stream to hit them. Then, my dear cats, we will see who laughs last! Nellie, turn the water off until I climb up and when I give the word turn it on again."

Up the ladder climbed Kittie, and sure enough when Nellie turned the water on it sent a shower that hit Button and nearly knocked him off the limb, while it also drenched Bella to the skin. She ran along the limb and tried to climb higher, but when Kittie saw what she was going to do, she turned the stream full on her and made her climb down the tree instead of going up. Then she soused Button from the tip of his nose to the end of his tail, and chased him down the same way. But when he got halfway down, he jumped and ran for home while Bella ran toward the barn and hid under it. Thus ended Button's adventure, as he related it to Stubby and Billy.

CHAPTER VIII

STUBBY TELLS WHAT HAPPENED TO HIM

Well," said Stubby, "my story isn't much to hear. You will have a good laugh over it, I suppose, though I can assure you what happened to me was no laughing matter.

"When we left here, Mr. Noland drove straight out into the country, and you must know he is a fast and reckless driver. I nearly bounced out of the car two or three times, for when he comes to a bad place in the road, instead of driving slowly he puts on more power and goes through lickety-split. As for turns and curves, I fell over on his lap every time he went around a corner. But the worst of it is he is very impatient if there is anything in the road that he can't pass. And it seemed to me I never saw so many pigs, chickens and slow-going farm wagons before. He would toot his horn, and the old farmers would not pay the slightest attention or give him one bit of the road, but just keep right on in the middle and jog along, giving us their dust. Mr. Noland would drive up close to their wagons and toot his horn until he would nearly break it. Then he would try to pass and nearly upset his machine in the deep ditches that bordered the road. But he always made it on two wheels, if not on four, and as he passed he would call out all sorts of things to the stupid old drivers. His favorite expressions were, 'Say, do you think you own the road?' and 'If you want to sleep, you better drive your old hayrack and rattling old bones to the side of the road,' or 'Now take a little of my dust and see how you like it!' And all the time he was growing madder and madder.

"Consequently when we came to some cows with one of them lying straight across the road and several others blocking the way as they stood about, I hopped out to drive them out of the way. But an old cow with a calf instead of running away from me as I supposed she would do, took after me and I was so busy dodging her that I did not notice another cow until I ran right into her. And she quickly lowered her head and hooked me out of the road and over the fence.

It was Stubby's and Button's frantic efforts to escape that had caused all the fun and laughter

"Now in this field was a flock of sheep quietly sleeping in the shade of a tree, an old ram with immense horns watching over them. I landed in the midst of the flock, which woke them up in a hurry and they jumped up and ran off, frightened almost to pieces at a strange dog falling in their midst. And the stupid things, instead of waiting to see if I was going to hurt them or not, all jumped up and ran baaing in all directions. This probably made the old ram, their leader, disgusted at them for being so foolish as to be afraid of so small a dog as I, and equally angry to think they had no more confidence in his ability to protect them from harm. And as they had all run off, so he could not vent his spite on them, he took it out on me and as I was looking for a place to crawl through the barbed wire fence he came up behind me and kindly butted me over.

"I must have made a funny picture hunting for a place to get through the fence, all unconscious of the old ram coming toward me and then being lifted over by a big butt. Anyway, when I landed in the middle of the road, I heard Mr. Noland laughing as if he would split his sides. And he called out, 'Excuse me for laughing at you, my little stubby-tailed dog, but I never saw anything so funny in my life! Hope you are not hurt, for I should hate to have you hurt when you were trying to do a favor for me. If another contrary old cow gets in the road, I'll run into her and boost her off the road myself.' Which he did later on, and this is what happened.

"He ran his car right into a cow in such a way that she sat on the bumper of the machine and he pushed her over on the bank. She slipped and fell back on the car and broke off one of the lamps. My, but he was mad! He threw stones at her and made me chase her for half a mile, calling out to me to bite her leg, bite her leg! This I did two or three times, but I only snipped her a little as I did not care to take any chances of being kicked sky high after having been butted twice in quick succession. My sides were still aching from the imprint of the cow's and the ram's horns.

"When we were again on the road and going along nicely, Mr. Noland said, 'Stubby, this seems to be a disastrous drive for us this morning, doesn't it?' He had scarcely gotten the words out of his mouth when bang! went a tire. Well, I would not like to repeat what he said. Now if there is anything he dislikes to do it is to put on a tire or fuss with the car in any way. He always manages to have either his son or the hired man do it. But here he was thirty-five miles from home on a road where few people passed.

"'I bet I haven't any inner tube to put in!' he muttered to himself, 'and even if I have, it is a mean job to fix it. I would run on the rim but if I do my whole wheel will be ruined. If I wait for some one to come and help me, I may wait until doomsday as this is a side road and little traveled.'

"He took off his hat, scratched his head and thought a minute. Then he climbed the fence at the side of the road and waved to a farmer he saw plowing in a field half a mile away. After many attempts he succeeded in attracting the farmer's attention, and he left his horses and came toward us. When he was within speaking distance, Mr. Noland called out, 'Mornin', Hiram! I am sorry to bother you, but I am in trouble. I have a busted inner tube and I can't fix it myself. Could you come and help me? The two of us can do it in a short time but it is an everlasting job for one to tackle. If you will help me, I'll give you a peck of that Golden Bantam seed corn you like so much the next time you are in town.'

"This corn was something Hiram had long coveted, as Mr. Noland's Golden Bantam corn is the envy of all the farmers as it is extra fine for table use. So Hiram jumped over the fence in a jiffy and the two set to work with a will. In twenty minutes the wheel was fixed and we were on our way.

"'That delay will make us reach our destination about dinner time, so we will have to ask them to keep us. I am right glad as Farmer Greenbush's wife is noted for her guinea pot pies, and perhaps if I hint around and flatter her, she might make one for our dinner. I'll just speed up a little until we get to the big Molkie Hill after which we can't make much time as the road is bad,' said Mr. Noland.

"For the next fifteen minutes we drove as fast as the little Ford would take us. Soon we were at the foot of the celebrated Molkie Hill. It is known far and wide as being the steepest and the most difficult hill for autos to climb for miles and miles around.

"'I'll just take it on a run,' said Mr. Noland to himself, and he put on full speed and we mounted to within a few feet of the top, when his engine stopped short and before he could put on his brakes we were running backwards down that hill at a terrific speed. When he did put on the brakes we were going so fast they did no good. Instead of him paying attention to his steering and keeping us in the middle of the road, he turned his head to see where he was going. I guess he lost his head and turned the steering wheel the wrong way, for we shot to one side of the road, hit the corner of the bridge at the bottom of the hill and turned upside down in the water. We knocked the top off, but otherwise we did not injure the car in the least."

"What became of you when the car turned over?" asked Button.

"I fell out as it went over and the current of the stream carried me from under it so I was not hurt. And Mr. Noland escaped too as the car caught in such a way on some rocks that it kept the body of the car from crushing him. As I swam out of the stream on the other side of the bridge, I saw him crawling out from under the wreck."

"Well, I should say you had had a very exciting morning," said Billy. "And how did you get home at last? I bet you lost your guinea pot pie though!"

"After Mr. Noland wiped some of the mud and dirt off himself, he sat on the bank a long time and did not say a word. I was beginning to get worried and was afraid he was hurt when he pulled out a memorandum book from his pocket and began to write in it. Presently he tore out a leaf and called me to come to him.

"'Come here, little dog. I want you to do something for me. I know you will if I can only make you understand what I want. Understand, only a very smart dog could do what I am going to ask you to do. Here is a note I want you to take to the store that is a mile from here over the top of this hill. You carry it in your mouth—or no, I'll tie it around your neck in my handkerchief. You take it to the storekeeper and bark. Then pull at the handkerchief with your teeth. He will think it is choking you and when he unloosens it he will find my note. After reading it he will hustle around and come to my rescue, bringing you back with him.'

"'Well, of all clever stunts to think of, this beats them all,' I thought.

"He placed the note carefully in the handkerchief and tied it around my neck. When it was fixed all right, I took a drink of water and started up the hill, while he called after me, 'Good luck, little dog; good luck!'

"In less than half an hour I was at the store, as it was easy to find. As I ran into the store, I found five or six big farmers loafing about or buying groceries or getting their mail. It was not hard to distinguish the storekeeper, as he was the only man without a hat and, besides, he stood behind the counter.

"Gee! It did smell good behind the counter for I was hungry and there were boxes of gingersnaps, crackers, Bologna sausage and all sorts of good things there. But I paid no attention to them as I wished to deliver my message. The storekeeper was a big, good-natured man, and he nearly stepped on me. In fact, he did nip my toe and I barked with the pain. This made him first look down and notice me.

"'Heigho! Here is a stray dog. I am sorry I stepped on you, but don't you know that customers are not allowed behind the counter?'

"Right here I rolled over on my back and began pulling the end of the handkerchief.

"'Mercy on us! The poor dog is going to have a fit! That handkerchief must be tied too tight. I'll just untie it. I wonder to whom he belongs? I thought I knew every dog for miles around.'

"He stooped down, and then, 'Bless my soul, there is something tied up in this handkerchief! I wonder what it can be?'

"When he found the note and had read it he called to the men in the store and read it to them.

"'Who brought the note?' asked one man.

"'No person brought it. This little dog carried it folded up in this handkerchief that was tied around his neck.' And he lifted me to the counter so all could see me.

"'Who but Noland would have thought of sending word in that way?' laughed another of the men.

"'Let's get a move on and all go to his rescue,' proposed a third.

"This they agreed to do, and soon five farmers were jogging along, ropes, pulleys and chains in the bottom of their wagons to help haul the wrecked car out of the stream.

"I was just about to jump off the counter and follow them when the storekeeper called out: 'Here, little dog, you must be hungry. Stop and eat a bite before you go back. You can easily overtake them.'

"He gave me a big lunch of sausage and a handful of crackers with butter on them, and three or four gingersnaps. I can tell you I blessed that good-hearted man for giving food to me. So few people ever seem to think that animals get hungry and thirsty, or they give them just a little piece of cake—not enough to stay the hunger of a tiny mouse. I licked up every crumb and wished as I did so that I had a pocket in my side so I could take Mr. Noland something to eat.

"'Say, little dog, do you suppose you could carry a sandwich or two back if I tied them on your back instead of around you neck? They would be too heavy to tie around your neck,' said the storekeeper.

"I barked and shook my head yes.

"'Well, I declare I believe this dog can almost talk, as well as understand all that is said to him!'

"Then he made two big sandwiches, one of Swiss cheese and the other of Bologna sausage, wrapped them in paper and tied them on my back with string and the handkerchief in which I had brought the note. Then he set a pan of nice cool water on the counter for me to drink. After this he put me on the floor by the door, where he stood watching me until I was out of sight.

"I can tell you Mr. Noland appreciated those sandwiches as much as I did the luncheon he had given to me. And he said to the farmers who were helping him, 'There is a good-hearted man and from now on I shall buy all I can at his store. He deserves to be helped.' To which all the farmers agreed and one and all said they traded with him altogether as they had found he never cheated on his weights or gave short measure.

"With the help of the farmers, the auto was soon up on the road and hitched to the back of one of the farm wagons that was going our way. Mr. Noland and I were in another wagon that was going the same way.

"In this manner we reached home just before dark. I tell you what; give me an auto in preference to a horse! My back fairly ached from trying to push those slow horses and it took hours to go over the road we had traveled in minutes by automobile.

"I am pretty tired, so I guess I will bid you both good-by and go to bed. Au revoir until to-morrow!"

"Not so fast!" said Button. "I am tired too, so I will turn in when you do."

"I am not feeling any too spry myself," said Billy. "So if you two are going to bed, I will also."

And presently the three Chums were fast asleep under the trees, living over again in dreams their experiences of the day.

CHAPTER IX

THE CHUMS RUN AWAY

The next day when Billy, Stubby and Button were resting on the grass on a side hill, Billy exclaimed in a petulant voice, "Say, fellows, I am getting tired of this place and I feel that it is time we were continuing our journey."

"I am exactly of that opinion," said Stubby.

"Anything you fellows plan is all right to me," said Button.

"Then it is agreed we move on," said Billy.

"The sooner the better for me," replied Button, "for I know I am in for a siege this afternoon when Nellie comes from school. I heard her ask Kittie to come over and bring Bella, and she said they would have a tea party under the trees, and make the cats sit in high chairs at the party, with bibs on their necks, and drink tea. 'Won't it be fun to see them sit up and drink tea?' she said.

"Now I have attended all the tea parties I want to, so unless we move on I shall have to find a place to hide all the afternoon."

"What do you say to starting this minute?" asked Billy.

"Say we do!" replied Stubby and Button as with one voice.

"In which direction shall we go?" asked Stubby.

"Toward the north, silly! Always toward the north, where home and Nannie are!" replied Billy.

"But the lake is north of us here," objected Stubby.

"I know it is, but we will follow its shore until we come to the end of it and then on north, or get a chance to cross the lake in a boat. And who knows but what we may come to a railroad track to follow which will be a short cut? Anyway, let's make for that high hill you see off there to the north and perhaps when we reach the top of it we can see a good road to follow."

"Well, here goes!" said Button, and he put his head down and started on a fast run, Billy and Stubby close at his heels.

They followed the lake shore as far as they could as it was better traveling there than in the high grass. They also kept as close to the water's edge as they could and still dodge the waves. Frequently Billy and Stubby were caught by a wave but they did not care as it only cooled them off. But Button contented himself by running along the wet sand out of reach of the waves.

They had gone about half a mile out of town and were still running along the beach when they came to a sawmill where there were a lot of men wading in the water up to their knees pushing the logs on to a narrow endless moving incline that carried them up into the mill where they would be sawed into lumber.

"Don't they look like big alligators being pushed up that plane to be killed?" said Billy.

"They really do, but I never thought of that before," replied Stubby.

"They remind me more of cattle being driven into the slaughter pens at the stockyards," said Button.

"There is something fascinating about watching those big logs being carried silently up into the mill to be turned into shingles, flooring and boards of various lengths to be made into furniture," remarked Billy.

"There surely is. But we can't stand here all day or we won't get far on our journey."

The three had just started on a run again when they heard a big voice which they recognized as Mr. Noland's calling to them. He stood on a tramway that ran from the mill to the boat landing.

"Here, you rascals, where are you going? And what are you doing so far from home? You'll get lost one of these days if you don't stop wandering around in a strange town the way you do. Here, come back, I say! Don't you hear me calling you? I just bet this old mill makes such a noise they don't hear me!" and he put his hands up to his mouth and tried to make a megaphone out of them, but it was of no avail. The Chums kept on at their rapid pace and turned neither to the right nor to the left, pretending they did not hear him.

After they were out of sight and sound of the mill, they stopped to rest and to get their breath for they had been running fast.

"I did not know Mr. Noland owned a mill, did you?" Billy asked.

"No. But he seems to own or at least have a hand in everything in that town, I have observed," said Button.

"I really think they will be sorry when they find we don't come back," said Stubby. "One could never find nicer people to live with. But we are too old travelers to settle down in any one place, no matter how nice it is. The wanderlust has surely got us by the throat."

"Billy," said Button, "you should go on a lecture tour through the U.S.A. and relate the different exciting experiences you have had in the many different countries you have visited."

"How about you and Stubby doing the same thing? You have been with me nearly everywhere I have been."

"I know, but you have so much more presence than we have and your voice carries so much further when talking than ours do," said Stubby.

"Just for sport I am going to enumerate some of the things that you could make into a dandy lecture," said Button. "You could begin with your experiences in the circus when you were young and before you were married. Then when you were hunting for the Kids the time they ran away and were carried off to Constantinople and you thought them dead. Next, some of the tales you told when you came home from Japan after being in the war between the Japanese and the Russians, and afterward how you found yourself down in Mexico. Next you could tell what you and your friends did along with Billy Junior, and your grandchildren, to say nothing of the scrapes you were in when you went on that memorable vacation and left Nannie at home. After that you could make a whole lecture on your hairbreadth escape in an aeroplane, what you saw in town and in Panama, on the Mississippi, in the West, at the World's Exposition in San Francisco, and last but not least in Europe during our Great War. And then you might end with our escape from France and the return to America. There would be a wonderful chance for a series of lectures and I bet before the audience heard them all their hair would be standing on end and they would be holding their breath from excitement at your many narrow escapes from death."

"There, Billy," said Stubby, "your life work is laid out for you. You travel and lecture while Button and I will be your press agents and go ahead and find a place for you to lecture in all the big cities and towns. If you did this, then Nannie could travel with you all the time. And I know you would both like that. Then too you would not grow so restless as it would keep you on the move all the time, for we would plan it so that you would give only three lectures in any one place and then go on to the next."

"The more I think of it, the more the idea appeals to me," said Button.

"Why not make our journey north into that kind of a trip right now?" said Stubby. "We could send word to Nannie to journey south to meet us."

"It does sound rather attractive," admitted Billy.

"Of course it does!" seconded Button. "And you owe it to the poor untraveled animals to give out some of your experiences to them, to enliven their humdrum lives and tell them about the outside world. Just see what a lot of pleasure the Dog and Cat Club give those stay-at-homes who have never been outside the suburbs of New York City — and most of them have never ventured ten blocks from where they were born."

"Hark!" exclaimed Billy. "I hear the most peculiar whistling, whizzing sound. It sounds up in the clouds, but I can't see a thing."

"It must be an aeroplane then, but I can't see a thing in the sky," said Button, but as he spoke a huge dirigible balloon poked its nose out of a cloud over their heads. It was so directly overhead that they could see every part of it distinctly.

"Isn't it a whale of a balloon? I never saw as large a one even in Europe," said Billy.

"Nor I either," said Stubby, full of wonder at its size.

"Look! It is slowly coming to earth. I believe they are going to land over in that clover field," said Button.

And sure enough they did. This great big dirigible, the first of its size to cross the Atlantic Ocean, was landing right before their eyes.

"Let us run over and get as near it as we can," Billy said.

When the monster airship landed, the Chums were not fifty feet away, and stood taking in everything as it slowly settled to earth.

Presently little windows and doors were seen to open in its sides and people came walking out. The Chums went nearer and found out by the conversation they overheard that they were forced to land as something was the matter with the machinery. The longer Billy looked, the more he wanted to see what the dirigible was like on the inside, until at last his curiosity got the better of him and he walked boldly up to the balloon and poked his head in one of the doors and gazed in. Not being driven away, or seeing any one, he stepped in and soon was exploring the balloon from one end to the other, with both Stubby and Button at his heels.

"Isn't it wonderful?" said Billy. "Just as cozy and nice as a ship that sails the sea. Staterooms, lounge, dining saloon, kitchen and storerooms galore! Let's hide and be carried off with her when she starts. It is worth being delayed on our journey to have such an experience."

"Indeed it is!" replied Button.

"Quick, get under that table! I hear some one coming," warned Stubby.

Billy dodged under the table in the dining saloon while Stubby hid under a chair and Button ran up a curtain and settled himself on the curtain pole near the ceiling. The person they had heard coming soon passed through the room, and they came out of their hiding places and continued their explorations.

Presently they found it difficult to stand on their feet, and looking from a window they discovered they were slowly rising from the ground. At the same time they found it was exceedingly hard to stand still and keep their balance. Before it should grow any worse, they ran back and hid where they had before, to await further developments.

"I hope if they find us they don't pitch us overboard when they get up two or three thousand feet," said Stubby.

CHAPTER X

UP IN A DIRIGIBLE

Help! Oh, help! I must have some air," whined Stubby. "I am getting seasick!" But neither Billy nor Button heard him as the noise of the engine and propellers drowned all other sounds in the balloon.

"If there was only a deck I could get out on! I wish I had not come! I just hate this way of traveling! It is worse than being in an elevator in a high building and having the car shoot from the bottom floor to the top in one bound. This thing is worse for it decides to stop, dropping and then shooting up again without warning, and it runs upside down and every other way but straight ahead. Oh, oh, oh! I can't stand it another minute. I must have air!"

So Stubby crawled out from under his chair and climbed up on a long, narrow window seat directly under an open window and hung out his head. He could only just reach the window by standing on his hind legs as he was so short and the window ledge was so far above the seat. As he looked out he could see the earth fast receding from him. He felt as if it were the dirigible that was standing still and the earth that was dropping from them. By this time they were so high in the air that the fields and forests looked like squares on a checkerboard and the broad rivers were mere silver threads across it. As for the churches and houses, they looked like card houses or toy paper villages. People he could see none; they were too small to be seen from this height. He became so interested looking that he forgot his seasickness, and he was very much surprised when they ran into a raincloud and he felt the raindrops on his face. But what surprised him most was to see lightning darting all around him and so near it seemed to go through the dirigible and come out the opposite side. As for the thunder, you people who have never been up in the clouds and heard it close at hand have no idea of the terrific noise and of the terror it causes one.

By this time the big dirigible was floundering in the stormclouds as a ship does in a heavy sea, only ten times more so. A dirigible is lighter than a ship and the wind at this altitude much stronger. It would catch the balloon up and carry it for miles out of its course on one of its fierce currents. Then without warning it would suddenly die down and the big balloon would drop hundreds of feet only to be caught up by another blast and twirled around or carried up again as the case might be, while constantly the lightning flashed and the thunder rolled and our Chums thought the very next gale would double them up and dash them to their death.

While Stubby was at the window, Billy was having his own troubles. He had tried to find a better place to hide than under the table and had come out to do so when an extra hard lurch of the balloon had sent him headlong the entire length of the dining saloon. He hit his head against the partition at one end of the room and then was flung back to the other end again. As the balloon was changing its course every minute, he could not regain his bearings. One minute the balloon would be standing almost perpendicularly, climbing to higher altitudes to try to get above the stormclouds. The next a heavy gust of wind would drive it back, or the gale would die down altogether and the dirigible would drop into a pocket of the atmosphere, or, worse yet, would be twirled around and around like a ship in a whirlpool of water.

Poor Billy went slipping head foremost from one end of the saloon to the other, sometimes sitting on his tail, at others rolling over and over until he felt like a jellyfish. But still the storm continued, and he could not find a place of safety.

As for Button, he had the best of it for when the balloon rolled or dove, he simply dug his claws further into the curtain pole and hung on for dear life. Once the dirigible sailed for hundreds of feet upside down. Button simply dug in deeper and hung upside down too.

The jerking of the dirigible knocked Stubby off the window seat and for many minutes he had been rolling from one end of the saloon to the other on one side of the table while Billy took the same journeys on the other side of the table, only it was not hurting Stubby so much as it was Billy. He had curled himself into a tight ball which made him roll easily. He looked like a ball of scraggly worsted. As for Billy, try as he would he could not curl up in a tight ball as his legs were too long and his horns much too sharp.

"Oh, my, will this storm ever be over? Why did we ever let our curiosity get the better of us and entice us to try a ride in this dangerous thing? No more dirigibles for me if I live to get out of this one, which I am very much afraid I won't!"

In less than five minutes from the time Billy thus spoke the dirigible had weathered the storm and was flying in clear blue sky a thousand feet above the still raging storm. They could still hear the thunder and see the vivid flashes of lightning.

"Gee! What a place to see the moon and stars," thought Billy. "Now the danger seems to be over, I wish we would stay away up here until dark so I could see what the moon and the stars look like when we are so near them. If we get near enough the moon, I should like to jump off and make a visit there."

Poor stupid Billy! He knew nothing of the thousands and thousands of miles between him and the moon, though it might look so very near.

When the dirigible was sailing quietly along, a waiter came in and began setting the table. He did not see our friends, and went whistling about his task. What most aroused the Chums' curiosity were the funny little fences he fastened on the table. Then when everything was ready, he sprinkled water on the tablecloth until it was quite wet.

"What in the world is he wetting that perfectly clean cloth for? I should like to know that," mused Billy. "I'll just watch and see."

Then before the waiter put down his sprinkling can, he took a plate and set it on the cloth to see if it was wet enough to keep the plate from slipping if the dirigible tipped or rolled to one side. Finding it was wet enough, he left the saloon and came back with a tray of goblets. These he fitted in holes made for them in the little railing that ran around the whole table.

"Well, I never!" exclaimed Billy. "Did you ever see anything as slick as that? Now the people won't have their plates or goblets slip into their laps as they eat. I wonder who ever thought of that scheme first. I should like to see how the kitchen looks. It must be as tiny as those on the Pullman cars. And I bet they have some new fandangled contraptions to keep the boilers of hot stuff and the frying pans from slipping off the stove when cooking. I'd go and try to get a peek at it but I'm afraid of being discovered and thrown overboard."

At this moment the waiter returned with a tray of spoons, knives and forks. As the swinging door closed behind him, he found himself facing a rolling ball of string coming straight toward him. As it reached his feet, he stepped to one side and the ball hit the door with such force that it flew open and the ball of string rolled through.

The waiter was so astonished that he braced himself against the partition while trying to catch his breath. As he stood there staring, he happened to glance up and there clinging to the curtain pole he saw a big, black cat staring back at him with wide open yellow eyes. This was too much for that waiter. He dropped the tray of silver and fled to the kitchen, but as the swinging door flew open to let him through, he bumped into the cook, who was in turn fleeing from the ball of string or worsted that was rolling around his kitchen floor, giving forth yelps like a dog. The two men clung to each other, their hair standing straight on end, and their knees knocking together.

As they stood thus, one of the officers of the dirigible having heard the racket as the silver fell to the floor, came in the saloon from the other end to discover what the trouble might be. Just then the craft gave a lurch which sent the folds of the tablecloth swinging out so that it disclosed Billy hiding underneath. The officer stared, wiped his eyes, and then stared some more.

At this moment Billy decided to come out and go through the door the officer was holding open.

When the officer saw a big, white goat rising from under the table he was so frightened that his legs shook together and he pulled the door shut. By this time Billy had up too much speed to slow down, so when his head hit the door he simply went through it as if it had been made of paper.

The noise of the splintering door brought the officer to his senses, and he called for help, but no one heard him. He was about to go to see where everybody was when the swinging door to the kitchen flew open and in rolled a yelping ball of string. At the same moment he spied Button staring down at him. He simply turned and fled to his berth, where he covered up his head so he could not see things, for he was fully convinced he was seeing things not of flesh and blood.

When Stubby in his mad rolling came to the door Billy had butted through, he bounded through the hole as a rubber ball might, and went bounding down the long narrow passage until he came up against a wall in a dark closet, as he supposed. But in reality he had rolled through an open door into the stateroom of the officer who had fled from Button and Billy, and had Stubby only known it at that very moment he was under his berth.

While all this had been taking place, the dirigible was fast descending toward its home hangar and in a few minutes they would be down to the earth again. And it was a good thing for the Chums that they were for when Billy was discovered by the Captain he ordered him thrown overboard with the dog and the cat. But if you think it an easy matter to catch as big and strong a goat as Billy with the fighting propensities he had and two lively animals like Stubby and Button, you are badly mistaken.

Two or three aviators tried to corner him and tie him up so they could pitch him overboard, but he butted and kicked so they could not lay hands on him. No more hands could be spared from the crew to help, as it required all the rest to manage the ship. Stubby and Button also put up a stiff fight as the men chased them all over the dirigible from under chairs and tables in this stateroom and that, where they upset things generally as the aviators tried to hit them with brooms, mops and whatever came handy.

While this was going on, the dirigible had quietly glided into its hangar and was quickly being tied up. An aviator was chasing Stubby with a long-handled brush when a man on the outside opened a door in the side of the dirigible just as Stubby was passing and quick as a wink he took advantage of it and jumped out, much to the surprise of the man who had opened it. After him came Button and Billy, and when the Chums' feet touched terra firma again they lost no time in leaving that aviation field. When they had found a nice, quiet, safe place to rest and were reviewing this last adventure, Billy said, "No more dirigibles for me! I never want even to see one again!"

"Nor I!" said Stubby. "I am one mass of black and blue bruises from hitting the furniture and door jambs as I rolled from one end of that long saloon to the other."

"And I still feel sick from hanging with my head down so long when that old dirigible traveled upside down," declared Button.

CHAPTER XI

THE OLD CROW CARRIES A MESSAGE TO NANNIE

After the Chums had rested and had a bath in a nearby lake, they lay down in a nice shady place to plan what they would do next.

"I think the first thing I should do," said Billy, "is to send a message to Nannie that the three of us are alive and well and are on our way to the old farm, and to ask her, Billy Junior, Daisy and the Twins to start for Chicago, where we will meet them in Lincoln Park as soon as we get there. It will take them as long to come the short distance from Fon du Lac to Chicago as it will take us to travel all the way from New York State, as they will have to travel slower, having the Twins with them. Besides, Nannie is not so young as she was and cannot stand the hardships of a hurried trip. I don't believe there is a carrier pigeon within a hundred miles of here to take my message, so I think I shall have to entrust it to the crows. There are crows in every State, and they are very reliable messengers and travel fast. One crow need not go all the way. One can carry it to the border of New York State, say, and there give it to another crow in Pennsylvania, and so on until it reaches my people in Fon du Lac, Wisconsin. If they get to Lincoln Park before we do, it is a fine place to wait as they can visit with the wild animals and get all the grass they want to eat in the Park, and all the water they want to drink and bathing too in Lake Michigan, which is on the east side of the Park. Now you fellows keep your eyes open for crows."

"I don't think we will see any around here," said Stubby, "as there is nothing they like to eat on the shores of this lake. We better find some cornfield, as we shall be sure to find plenty of crows there."

So the three got up and trotted along until they came to a cornfield. And sure enough, the first thing they saw was a big, black crow sitting on a scarecrow as unafraid as if it had been a tree. On seeing this, Billy exclaimed,

"That is the crow for me! He has no fear and will let nothing turn him from his way. I am going to ask him to carry the message."

"Aren't you ashamed of yourself to take the baby's bottle away from it!" reproved Nannie

Saying this, Billy jumped the fence that encircled the cornfield, and approached the crow.

Crows not being afraid of animals, the old fellow on the scarecrow did not stir as Billy approached, but when he was within twenty feet of him, the crow cawed out:

"Well, I never! If this isn't my old friend Billy Whiskers! And how do you come to be away down East, when I met you away out West years ago?"

"You don't mean to tell me that you are Black Wings, that saucy dandy who carried a message for me once from Salt Lake City, Utah, to Fon du Lac, Wisconsin?" gasped Billy.

"I surely do! I am that very crow, only no longer young or dandified."

"From your looks I should say the world had treated you fine," said Billy.

"Look who is here—Stubby and Button, the same traveling companions you had with you in the West!" exclaimed the crow in astonishment.

"Fellows, hurry your bones and see who is here," baaed Billy to Stubby and Button.

"Don't tell me it is Black Wings!" barked Stubby, while Button meowed, "You have grown portly since I saw you last, and are much more eatable looking than you were then, though you looked very good to me that day I was starving and tried to catch you to eat." And they all laughed, for once Button had nearly caught Black Wings, but he proved too quick for the half starved cat and flew up in a cactus plant and cawed and scolded Button. Afterwards they became good friends, and Black Wings carried a message to Nannie telling her that Billy, Stubby and Button would be back at the old farm on Billy's birthday. They had met the crow on the desert near Salt Lake City, and he had flown over them and showed them where there was an oasis on the desert, affording food and water that was not alkaline. After which he carried the message straight to Nannie without a relay as he was going East and said he would as soon go to the old farm as anywhere else.

"I should be delighted to carry another message for you. I always like to do a friend a favor when I can. Besides, I should enjoy seeing your sweet wife, handsome son and cunning grandchildren again. I shall never forget the rousing party they gave me, and the amount of corn I ate that night. I really ate so much I thought my skin would burst. Now what is the message you wish me to take this time? And I suppose you are in a tearing hurry as you usually are?"

"No; this time I am in no hurry at all, as there will be plenty of time for you to go there and get back before we can possibly reach Chicago. All I wish you to do is to go to the farm you went to before and tell Nannie that we three Chums have returned from the War safe and sound and without losing an eye or a leg, and for her to meet us in Chicago. Ask her too to bring as many of the family with her as she can induce to come, and for them to meet us in Lincoln Park as it is the safest and most comfortable place I can think of for them to wait for us. And also tell her to allow a month for us to get there as we might be captured and shut up somewhere for a time. But it will be only for a time; no one could keep us long."

"Now if you fellows would like, I can show you an easy road to travel that will take you to Chicago by the shortest and quickest route. Do you see that line of telegraph poles the other side of this field? Well, just follow them until you come to the first town. When you get there, leave them and follow the railroad. It will take you straight into Chicago, but be careful you don't get on a side track when going through some of the cities and towns where many railroads meet. All the way along you will find good friends and farmhouses where you can rest and get something to eat. I see a man with a gun coming this way. He has not seen us yet, but he soon will, so I guess we better say good-by and separate."

Bing, bing, bang! and a shot went clear through the crown of the old straw hat on the scarecrow where the crow had just been sitting.

CHAPTER XII

BILLY WHISKERS' FAMILY START FOR CHICAGO

Two weeks from the time the old crow took the message from Billy, he delivered it to Nannie early one morning when she had just awakened from a sound sleep on the top of a straw stack. It was her usual resting place, for from this vantage point she could get a view of all the country roundabout as the stack stood on the top of a high hill. Here she spent most of her time night and day when Billy was away, looking for him to return. From here she could see not only the country roads, but also the railroad as well as the meadows and woodland. Consequently from whichever direction Billy might come she would be the first to see him. It was from this very lookout she had seen him when he returned from his western trip, from his Panama expedition and from across the ocean and far-away Constantinople. You must not forget that Billy was a traveled goat.

This particular morning she awoke at sunrise, but seeing a heavy mist hid the sun, she tried to go to sleep again as it foretold a hot day. But just as she was dropping off to sleep, she heard a crow caw directly over her head, and she thought it queer that the crows would be stirring so early. Again she closed her eyes to sleep, but the call was repeated and it sounded so much nearer than at first that she opened her eyes once more. Lo and behold! directly in front of her on a dead limb of a tree sat a big, black crow.

"Don't you know me, Mrs. Billy Whiskers?" cawed he.

"It isn't—it can't be our old friend and messenger Black Wings!"

"That is just who it is! You have good eyes, Mrs. Whiskers, to recognize me after all these years, especially as they say I have grown stouter."

"That you surely have, but any one having once seen your sharp, shrewd eyes would never forget them or the saucy turn of your head. You can't be here to give me another message from my beloved husband, can you?"

"That is just my business—to deliver a message from him, to tell you that he, Stubby and Button are all well and happy and, best of all, that none of them lost so much as an eye or a leg in the War. Which is quite remarkable, I think, as they were in the thick of the fight more than once, and were also torpedoed by a submarine. But just wait until you see them! They themselves will tell you about their war experiences."

"Oh, how happy you have made me, Mr. Black Wings, by bringing me the message that the husband I adore is safe and sound and in this country once again! I don't believe I can ever stand it to have him go away from me again. I have died a thousand deaths in imagining him wounded and left to die on the battlefield, or, worse yet, blown to atoms by a shell. Come with me while I tell Billy Junior and Daisy the good news."

And Nannie slipped off the straw stack and went to where Billy Junior, his wife Daisy, and their Twins were asleep at the foot of a haystack in the barnyard.

"Why, mother! Are you ill?" asked Billy Junior when he awoke and saw her standing over him.

"No, dear. But I have such good news for you that I could not wait for you to awaken, but had to come and tell you. Hurry and get your eyes open and see who is here!"

"Not father, surely?"

"No; but an old friend who has brought news of him."

Billy Junior rubbed his face against his fore leg to get the sleep out of his eyes, so he could see who was there. At first he looked and looked, but he saw no one. He was looking on the ground, and Black Wings was perched on the tongue of an old farm wagon not ten feet away. When he saw the blank expression on Billy Junior's face, he cawed to show him where he was.

"Black Wings!" Billy exclaimed when he saw him. "How glad I am to see you once again! You should be called White Wings instead of Black Wings as you always bring such bright, cheerful news. Mother says you have good news for us. I can guess that it must be from father."

"You are right; it is. He is sound and well, and is coming to see you just as fast as his four legs can carry him. And Stubby and Button are with him. He sent me on ahead to tell you that he would like to have you, your mother, wife and the Twins join him in Chicago. You will have plenty of time to get there as they are away down East yet, in the state of New York. But though they are farther away from Chicago than you are, they can travel faster than you can, having the Twins with you."

"But how shall we ever be able to find him in such a large city as Chicago?" asked Nannie.

"He has instructed me to tell you to meet him in Lincoln Park, for should you arrive first, that will be an interesting place to wait as there are all the wild animals to talk to and plenty of good green grass in the Park to eat, and cool, clear water to drink as it borders on Lake Michigan."

"What are you talking about?" asked one of the Twins. "Going on a journey? We want to go too!"

"We both want to go!" piped up the other Twin. "We haven't been off this old stupid farm for ages, and I am crazy to go on a journey and talk to all the little lambs and goats along the road."

"Keep still, children! Don't you see Mr. Black Wings is telling us what Grandfather wants us to do?"

"Oh, I bet it is something bully if he is planning it," said one Twin.

"Bet your sweet life it is!" chimed in the other.

"Children, how many times must I tell you not to use such language?" said their mother. "If you don't behave, we will leave you at home."

"You can't do that. Grandfather told you to bring us and he would be disappointed if you did not."

"Hush! Don't be impertinent!"

"You have all been to Chicago so will know the way," remarked Black Wings.

Just then a rooster flew up on the wagon to crow that it was daylight and time for all the barnyard animals and fowls to be up and licking their coats or preening their feathers, which is what they do each morning instead of washing their faces as little boys and girls do.

"Mr. Chanticleer," called Nannie, "won't you crow out an invitation to all the animals and fowls to come to the spring at the foot of the barnyard as soon as they are up, to meet Mr. Black Wings? He has just come with a message from Billy, my husband, that he has landed in America safe and sound and is on his way here with our old friends Stubby and Button."

"With pleasure. Mrs. Whiskers! And I will crow my loudest and longest, for nothing in this world would give me more happiness than to welcome our old chum and friend back to the farm."

"Mother," said Mr. Winters, the owner of the farm, "that rooster will split his throat if he doesn't stop crowing so loud and long. He doesn't generally keep it up so long. If he continues to crow like that in the mornings when I wish to sleep, we will roast him for Sunday dinner."

About an hour later when Mr. Winters went to the farmyard, as he did each morning, to take a look around before breakfast, he was surprised to see all the animals congregated around the spring. Even the pigs, chickens, ducks and turkeys were there.

"Strange they should all be so thirsty this morning," he pondered. "If I had given them salt last night, I might have thought it was that but they haven't had any for days. Heigho! there goes an old crow, the first I have seen around here for ages."

When the animals saw Mr. Winters they all separated and wandered off in a careless manner. As soon as Mr. Winters had returned to the house, you could have seen, had you been looking, three big goats and two young ones hurrying down the lane that led from the barnyard to the main road to Chicago, with a big, black crow flying over them.

CHAPTER XIII

BILLY WHISKERS' FAMILY ARRIVE AT LINCOLN PARK

After numerous hardships and accidents of all kinds, the Billy Whiskers family arrived in Lincoln Park. The first thing they did was to go straight to the bathing beach to wash the stains of travel off their coats before visiting the animals.

They reached the Park three days before Billy could possibly have gotten there, and they were proposing to pass the time until his arrival by sightseeing and talking to the animals in the cages, but they came near being captured and shut up the very first day they were there. It happened in this way.

When they reached the beach there were only a few people in the water and lying on the sand, as it was too early in the day for the crowd, though those who were there made up in noise and fun for those who were not.

The lifeguards were lazily lounging in their boat away from shore when they heard an angry scream from some woman in the water. They thought some one must be annoying her, but on looking up they saw her swimming for shore as fast as she could go, while on the sand stood three black goats and two white ones beside a two-year-old baby lying on a shawl, kicking and screaming. Over it stood a small goat with the baby's bottle dangling from its mouth as it chewed the rubber tubing, while the other young goat was eating some sweet cakes it had found in a bag, and one of the old goats was licking the baby's forehead. That was Daisy, the Twins' mother. She meant no harm as this was her way of kissing the sweet little baby. Daisy loved babies and she thought this would quiet this little child. Billy Junior tried to get the bottle away from the Twin to give back to the baby so it would not cry.

"Aren't you ashamed of yourself to take the baby's bottle away from it!" reproved Nannie.

"But I was thirsty and wanted a drink of milk!"

"Never mind if you did. You should not take it away from a tiny baby."

"He isn't very tiny! Just hear how he yells!"

By this time the baby's mother had reached the spot and was throwing stones and sand at the goats while she tried to pacify the baby.

As the goats saw the lifeboat head for the shore, they thought they better disappear, knowing that the minute the men beached the boat they would be after them. So they raced into the Park and hid themselves behind some lilac bushes. Daisy said:

"I really don't see why you children don't behave. You have done nothing but get into mischief and cause us trouble ever since we left home. I wish we had not brought you! Any one would think you never had any bringing up. And now to try to take a sweet little baby's dinner away from it! I am ashamed of you! Besides, now none of us can take a bath on that nice sandy beach. We shall have to find another place, which won't be very easy since the lifeguards have seen us."

"I know where there is a nice little lake, mamma," piped up one Twin. "I saw it as we came along—right over there where you see that high bridge."

"Very well. We will all go over there for I feel very dirty and tired. It will both clean us and rest us to have a nice cool bath."

So the goats all trotted over to one of the lagoons in the Park which the Twins had called a lake, and they plunged into the water. They had a fine time and enjoyed themselves, much to the discomfort of some stately swans that were greatly upset to have strange goats come dashing into their private place. They began to hiss, which set all the ducks to quacking and the sea lions to barking. This commotion soon brought a park guard to the spot to see what was the matter. When he discovered a lot of goats in the water he walked down to the edge of the pond and began to wave his club and shout at them.

"Hear the old goose!" said one of the Twins. "He is shooing at us! I guess he thinks we are a kind of duck!"

"Let's baa at him, and tell him what an old goose he is," said the other.

Oh, oh! Where did you come from?" wailed one little girl when the kids jumped out of the shrubbery and grabbed her bag of popcorn

When the goats did not leave the water or pay any attention to him, the guard began throwing stones at them. At last one hit Billy Junior on the head. This was too much for him. The guard might throw stones all he wished, but hitting Billy Junior with them was quite another thing. He wheeled and swam for shore, going straight for the guard, who stood still, not knowing Billy Junior was bent on butting him.

Indeed Billy Junior did butt the guard so hard he sent him flying over the high iron fence that surrounded the sea lions' pool and rock cave where they lived. He fell kersplash into the water, astride a papa sea lion as he went swimming round and round his rock home. When the lion felt something alight on his back, he dove to the bottom of the pool in a flash, taking the guard with him. But no human being could stick on the back of a slippery sea lion, and the guard soon came up to the surface of the water blowing and spouting like a porpoise.

The goats did not wait to see what became of the guard but ran and hid themselves under the approach of one of the Park bridges.

CHAPTER XIV

THE TWINS ARE LOST

Early the next morning before the crowds of people began to come to the Park, the goats had a fine time visiting all the animals, going up one path and down another and in one animal house and out another until they came to the lions' cages. These roaring, ferocious beasts with their glaring yellow eyes, tawny manes, big red mouths and gleaming teeth frightened the Twins nearly into spasms and they ran away from the family so fast that their mother could not follow them. They dodged under this bush and that, around curves in the paths and behind the animal cages so quickly that she gave up the chase and came back to get their father to help her.

"They have gone and we can't catch up to them now," said he. "Stay here and go with us a bit and when we have seen all the animals we wish to see, I'll look for them. They will be frightened after a while when they find they are alone, and begin to hunt us," said their father.

So Billy Junior, Daisy and Nannie walked leisurely from cage to cage, saying a word here and a word there to all the animals and birds they saw. And this is how it happened that the Twins found themselves alone in the Park.

"Gee! I hope those big beasts don't break out of their cage and come after us! We would only make one mouthful for them and I bet they like tender kid meat at that!" shuddered one Twin.

"Don't even mention it!" said the other. "I can feel my bones crunch in their big mouths and see them lick their chops after they have eaten us."

"Where shall we go now? We can do as we please all day if we just keep out of sight of the family."

"We'll keep our eyes open for them, never mind, and if we see them coming, we will hide. I wonder what is in that big cage over there? I see something flying from one side to the other but it doesn't look like a bird. Let's go see what it is."

So they trotted off and soon found themselves in front of the monkeys' cage.

"Oh, look, look! Aren't they the funniest looking things you ever saw? They have faces like a baby or an old man and tails like a cat!"

"See that big one away up in that perch holding a little teeny, tiny one in its arms just as a woman holds a baby!"

"One of them has its tail sticking out of the cage. Wait until I go pinch it with my teeth and see what it will do."

Cautiously the little mischief crept up to where the big monkey was sitting with his back to them, tail swinging outside the cage. But the Twin pinched it harder than he meant to, and the next thing he knew his head was being banged against the bars of the cage and the monkey was trying to pull him through the bars by his short horns.

The only thing that really saved the Twin was that his horns were short and slippery and the monkey could not hold on to them. Seeing this, he let go to grab hold of the kid's ears, but he was not quick enough, for just as he let go one horn the kid gave a lurch and fell to the ground. It took but a second for him to regain his feet and baa for his brother. But what was his dismay to see his brother running down the path like mad, trying to shake off a tiny monkey that was sitting on his back!

While one Twin had been biting the big monkey's tail, the other had been watching a baby monkey squeeze itself between the bars of the cage and escape. But he never would have watched had he known what that little monkey intended doing when he got out. It was this: to get a ride on the kid's back, for it had no sooner slipped through the bars of the cage than it made a bound and landed on the kid's back. As its claws dug into his flesh, he kicked and butted to shake it off, but it only clung the tighter.

"You'll stick to my back in spite of me, will you? Well, we'll see!" and off the kid started for a duck pond near by. He was in the water and swimming for the opposite shore before the monkey realized what had happened. He could not jump off now as he did not know whether he could swim or not, this being the first time he had ever been near water. He did not know that all animals can swim by instinct.

He chattered and called in monkey language for the ducks and the geese to save him, but they were much too busy saving themselves from this stranger in their pond to give him any help, and they flew squawking in all directions. At last after the kid had dived two or three times and the monkey had come up with his eyes and mouth full of water, he decided to jump onto the back of one of the geese or swans when he got near enough one. Just then a stately swan that had refused to be frightened or even disturbed by the entrance of the kid in his particular pond sailed majestically by with his head up, neck curved and wings slightly raised to show them off to the very best advantage.

"That is a good safe place for me," thought the little monkey. "I'll jump and sit on that swan's back between his wings. They will shelter me and keep me from falling off."

As the swan approached the kid, it hissed a warning for him to get out of the pond. His second hiss died in his throat with surprise when the monkey landed on his back. At first the swan was too much taken back to do anything but sail on by the kid, but when he had collected his senses, he tipped himself upside down with head and half his body under water, and remained in this position so long that the monkey fell off and had to swim for shore.

When he came out of the water, he happened to come out beside the kid, who stood shaking himself. He stopped in a hurry when he saw the half drowned little monkey coming out of the pond looking more like a drowned rat than a monkey. He did not wait to give himself another shake, but dove into the water and swam for the place where he had first entered the pond, and there he found his Twin awaiting him, laughing as if his sides would split.

"Come along! We must hurry away from here before we have hissing geese and quacking ducks bring the guards down on us. I smell sweet peas! Let's go eat some. I just love the blossoms—they are sweet as honey."

People driving along the parkway thought it strange that the Park commissioners would allow goats to run loose through the flower beds and pull the sweet peas off their trellises. Had they driven by a few minutes later they would have enjoyed the fun of seeing a big fat guard as broad as he was long, a long handled rake in his hand,trying to drive two innocent looking kids out of those very same flower beds.

They were too spry for him, however, and when he drove them out of one bed they simply ran into another and stood eating until he was again within striking distance of them. Then they would scamper away and begin on another bed. They did this until the man was so angry that his face was as red as a turkey cock's, while his breath came in gasps. At last he tripped over the hose and fell sprawling in a puddle of water. This, however, gave him an idea, and he determined to turn the water on the kids. Up he got and without looking to see if they were still there, he turned the hose where they had stood but a second before. But alas! the stream of water hit his best girl who was walking between two of the flower beds pushing a baby carriage. The kids were nowhere in sight!

"Oh, Rosy, Rosy, forgive me, forgive me! I thought you was a goat!"

"So I look like a goat, do I, you miserable old clumsy fellow, you! Take that—and that—and that!" as she struck him over the head with one of the baby pillows, and then began to cry. Blinded by her tears, she pushed the baby carriage right over the flower beds, heedless of where she was walking, sobbing, "He thought I was a goat! I don't look like a goat, I don't! Boo hoo hoo!"

By this time the gardener had collected his wits enough to go to her and explain. The last the kids saw of them as they bounded away, he had his arm around her and was loving her, much to the amusement of passersby.

"I smell something good," said one of the Twins.

"So do I! Let's go see what it is."

"It comes from over by that big red brick building."

They trotted over and found it came from a popcorn wagon.

"Yum, yum! It is popcorn with butter and salt on it!"

"Oh, I just love it, don't you?"

"Yes, but I like it best with chocolate on it. Wait until the man who owns the stand is not looking and then we will run up and grab a bag."

"I know a safer plan. Here come two little girls with bags in their hands. One has a bag with buttered corn in it and the other has one with chocolate poured over the corn. I saw the man fixing it for them. We will hide behind these bushes and when they are opposite us we will jump out, grab the bags and run. Which girl do you think has the buttered corn and which the chocolate?"

"The girl with the pink bow has the buttered corn, so you take her bag, while I go for the other one."

"Oh, oh! You horrid things! Where did you come from?" wailed one little girl when the kids jumped out of the shrubbery at her and grabbed her bag of chocolate popcorn.

The other little girl held onto her bag and began to run, holding it high above her head, but she squeezed the bag so tightly that it broke and the corn scattered on the ground. Then the kid quickly gathered up a great mouthful and ran off.

The little girl went wailing to a park policeman and told him her troubles and the kids saw him turn and run toward them. They raced off, chewing the paper bags as they ran, seeking a good place to hide, which they found in a thick clump of lilac bushes. After devouring the very last bit of paper that had either butter or chocolate sticking to it, they fell asleep. And here they were found by the night watchman who carried them off and shut them in a pen with some Angora goats from across the sea.

CHAPTER XV

THE ELEPHANTS ARE ENRAGED AT THE GOATS

Billy Junior, Daisy and Nannie visited the cages of all the animals, and gave no more thought to the runaway Twins until hour after hour went by and the Twins did not come back. Neither had they seen them playing in the Park and Daisy began to grow nervous about them. At last she said to her husband,

"Billy, I can't stand this suspense any longer. I am beginning to fear that something has happened to the Twins. You know they might have wandered over to the lake and been drowned. You and Nannie may go on calling on the different animals, but I am going to hunt for the kids."

"You are quite right," said Nannie. "I have been uneasy about them for some time, but did not like to mention it for fear of alarming you. We will go with you and help hunt for them."

"Yes," agreed Billy Junior, "it is high time we were finding them. There is no knowing what they might do, they are so daring and mischievous. We'll outline a systematic plan for the hunt. Each one will go in a different direction and scour all the paths in that section of the Park, looking around every cage that we see. Then when the clock strikes twelve we will meet in front of the yard where the elephants are kept."

Billy Junior went to the south, Nannie to the east and Daisy to the north.

Every step Daisy took, she grew more worried, and when she passed a cage of ferocious tigers and panthers who she knew lived on kid meat, she shivered to think that perhaps they were licking their chops because they had just finished eating one of her darlings who in some way might have squeezed between the iron bars of their cage.

On, on she went, her knees knocking together from fear and fatigue, when she thought she heard their voices calling, "Mamma! Mamma!"

She hastened in the direction from which the sound came and there, sure enough, shut up in a yard with other goats she saw her two darling babies. There was no mistaking them as they were the handsomest kids you ever saw, one being white as snow like Daisy and the other black as night like its father, Billy Junior.

"Oh, my darlings, my darlings!" she called when she saw them, and both kids came running to the fence to be kissed on the ends of their saucy little noses which they stuck through the bars of the iron fence. "Where have you been and how does it come you are shut up here?"

"Oh, mamma, get us out for we are afraid of that big, horrid black goat over there with the great horns. He said if we did not stop calling for you, he would hook us over the moon with his big horn."

"Who said they would hook you?" asked Billy Junior, who had just come up to the fence with Nannie.

"That old fellow over there asleep by the house," said one Twin.

"I should like to see him try to do it. If he did, he would see himself flying over the moon," said Billy angrily.

While the goats had been talking to the kids, several men with rakes and pitchforks in their hands had come up behind them and formed in a semicircle. Hearing a crunching of the gravel on the walk behind him, Billy looked around and knew in a second that they were trapped. There was no use of trying to fight men armed with pitchforks, so when they began to drive them toward an open gate that led into the pen where the kids were, Daisy, Nannie and Billy Junior showed no fight, but went quietly as lambs. After the men had left, Billy Junior said,

"Well, this is a pretty how-de-do! Here we are locked up and father coming to see us after being away two years. Now we can't greet him except through the bars of a fence! It really is too bad. We should have had sense enough to leave the kids at home, knowing as we do how mischievous they are."

They were shut in this pen three days and were growing heartily sick of the monotony of walking around their small yard in the daytime and being shut in a stuffy little room at night with the other goats who paid little attention to them.

"If that fence were not so very high, I could jump it," said Billy Junior. "But should I try and fail, I might fall back on the long, sharp spikes and hang there."

"Or if only the bars were not so close together, we would starve ourselves and squeeze through," remarked Daisy.

"Or dig under," suggested Nannie, "if the bars did not go down into the ground so far."

"Oh my, oh my, oh me! Isn't this life awful, with nothing to do but wander around this old yard where the grass is all tramped down and burnt by the hot sun, with people walking by and looking at you all the time? Only an occasional kind-hearted person gives you a peanut or the core of an apple," grumbled Billy Junior.

"I wish your father were here," said Nannie. "When everything looked hopeless, he always found a way out."

"So do we wish he was here," chimed in Daisy and Billy Junior.

"Mercy sakes alive!" exclaimed Daisy the next moment. "See where those kids are! In the elephant yard!" and she jumped to her feet and ran to the fence which separated the yard where the goats were confined from that of the elephants. "How did you two get over there?" she asked severely. "Come straight out of that yard! The elephants may not like kids and kill you."

"You are perfectly correct, madame," said an elephant. "I dislike goats of all kinds, and so would you if in my place. Forced to live month in and month out next to a goat pen where the disagreeable odor all goats have is carried to my nostrils until I am sick from it and cannot eat is far from pleasant."

"Did I hear you say," said Billy Junior, stepping up beside his wife, "that you do not like the smell of goats?"

"That is exactly what I did say," replied the elephant. "And I will repeat it if you wish me to do so."

"Oh, don't take the trouble! Saying it once is enough. But allow me to inform you that the odor of a goat is as sweet to the nostrils as roses and lilies compared to the odor from an elephant. That resembles the smell from a garbage pile!"

Now Billy Junior had done it! The elephant became enraged and tried to break down the fence between them. When he found he could not do this, he trumpeted and pawed the earth, throwing great clods of dirt all over them.

"Come out of there! Come out of there!" called Daisy to the kids. "He will kill you!"

But the Twins could not get out as the elephant was between them and the hole through which they had crawled. Seeing them, he charged but he was so big and they so small that they simply ran between his legs when he tried to catch them up with his trunk.

Daisy, Nannie and Billy Junior all stood panic-stricken at the chances the kids took. First they would run under his body from side to side, then between his hind legs. Had he moved a foot, they would have been crushed between his great legs. There being two of them and both so small and frisky, they confused the beast so he did not think as quickly as usual. He had been out of the jungle for years where he had had to think fast, and now he found himself rusty and unable to cope with frisky little pests like these two kids.

"I'll fix them," he said to himself, and he walked over to where his tub of drinking water stood, and filled his trunk. Then he charged down on the Twins where they stood in one corner, waiting to see what he would do next. The little rascals were enjoying the rage of the elephant very much and were not afraid of him at all as they thought they could trust to their wits to save themselves.

The elephant walked up to within five feet of them. Then he stopped and squirted the water at them with such force that it knocked one of them over when it hit him broadside. The other kid it blinded so he could not see where to run. Then they heard a bellow of rage and pain. Shaking the water from their eyes, they saw a big white goat run under the elephant's stomach and scratch the skin with his short horns so badly that it made the monster cry out with pain and turn to see what had attacked him so suddenly. When he faced about whom should he see but old Billy Whiskers himself in front of him. At the same moment he felt a cat on his back and a dog snapping at his heels.

But what had changed the enraged elephant so quickly? For now he was as docile as a lamb, and the kids saw him go up to Billy and wind his trunk around Billy's beard and playfully pull it, at the same time saying,

"Billy Whiskers! My old friend Billy Whiskers of the circus! Where by all that is wonderful did you come from? I supposed you were dead long ago."

Elephants live to be over a hundred years old, but goats not so long, and as it had been many years since these two had traveled and performed in the same circus, the elephant had taken it for granted that Billy was dead.

"Excuse me a minute until I throw out these smelly young kids. I can't stand their odor," said the elephant.

"If you don't mind, I will put them out myself, as I think I can do it more gently than you could, and I happen to have an interest in those particular kids as they are my well beloved grandchildren whom I have not seen for two years," replied Billy.

"Your grandchildren!" exclaimed the elephant. "I beg your pardon. Had I known they were related to you in the most distant manner, I would not have harmed a hair of their skin. I do hope you will forgive me!"

"Certainly I will forgive you. And perhaps they were annoying you and deserved being punished, for as I remember them they were pretty mischievous kids."

"Take after their grandfather, eh?" said the elephant.

"I guess so," said Billy.

"Baa, baa, baa!" came a voice as sweet as music to Billy's ears and turning he saw his darling wife looking through the fence.

"How did you get shut in there?" he asked. "I'll be with you in a minute!" But though he looked and looked he could find no opening leading into the yard where Nannie was confined. He had gotten into the elephant's yard by jumping through an open window in the elephant's house and running out the door that led to the yard, and Stubby and Button had followed him. Billy had recognized the kids, and seeing them in danger he had not stopped to figure how they got there, but had rushed to their rescue immediately. He and Stubby and Button had just arrived in the Park after their long journey from New York State, and were looking for the family when they chanced to turn a corner in the path and came upon this scene.

The kids slipped back into the goat yard the way they had left it, while Billy, Stubby and Button stood and talked to Nannie, the fence between them.

"Oh, if I could only find a way to get over into your yard," baaed Billy to Nannie.

"I have it!" said the elephant. "I can get you all over there if you don't mind being dropped a few feet."

"Certainly we don't, but how are you going to do it?"

"I'll just pick you up with my trunk and drop you on the other side of the fence."

"You can't do it," said Billy. "I am too heavy."

"Indeed, I can do it! I guess you are no heavier than the mahogany logs I used to lift and put in high piles when I lived in Siam. Come here and let me try."

The elephant encircled Billy's body with his trunk and lifted him up from the ground and over the fence as easily as if he had been a feather. When he had raised Billy to the top of the fence, he unwound his trunk and dropped him over into the next yard where his family awaited him.

When the elephant turned to get Stubby and Button to put them over the same way, he found they had crawled through the hole the kids had used.

Such a smelling of noses, and licking of faces you never saw as when the Billy Whiskers family and their friends were once again reunited after this long separation while Billy had been in the war in Europe.

"Isn't it too bad, my dear," said Nannie, "that we are all shut up in this yard with no hopes of getting out? And I was just saying to Daisy that if you were here, you would soon find a way to secure our freedom."

"And I shall, my dear. I shall just wait until the keeper comes in through the gate to look after the goats. Then I shall either butt him over as he comes in or butt down the gate when he takes the padlock and chain off. Anyhow, I shall find a way to get us out of here very soon, I am sure. Now we will think only of the present and enjoy every minute of being together. What fine kids the Twins have grown to be! But I imagine they are just as mischievous as ever."

"Can you wonder at it when you stop to consider who their father and grandfather are?" said Nannie.

"Gracious! What can be causing all that commotion over in the farther corner of the yard, I wonder?" said Daisy.

"Where are the Twins?" asked Billy Junior.

"I don't know," answered their mother.

"Then I guess you will find that they are at the bottom of the fracas over there. I'll go see," said their father, and off he trotted to find out if the kids were in mischief.

Presently he came back, driving both kids before him. But what had happened to them? They were as dirty as dirty could be and both were crying.

"Oh, my precious darlings!" exclaimed Daisy. "Who has been hurting you?"

"No one has been hurting them. They need a good spanking! Where do you think I found them? In the middle of a ring of Angora goats, having a fight with two kids about their own size. It would have been all right to have had a boxing match, but they did not play fair. They lost their tempers and when they got the other kids down, they hooked and tramped them unmercifully. I don't like that! They must fight fair and keep to the rules of boxing, and not beat up their adversaries when they are down."

"Come here, kids," said their grandfather. "If you will promise to be good all the rest of the day, I will tell you a story of the Great War and of some of the things that happened to Uncle Stubby and Uncle Button and myself when fighting in the army."

CHAPTER XVI

A PANTHER ESCAPES FROM THE CAGE

The Billy Whiskers family as well as all the Angora goats were enjoying themselves listening to Billy, Stubby and Button tell war stories, when they noticed great excitement among the people in the Park, who began running in all directions, screaming as they ran.

"What can the matter be?" they asked one another. "I'll go over by the fence that leads along the walk," suggested Billy, "and listen and see if I cannot find out what is frightening the people so. Something important must have happened for they all look so scared and palefaced."

All the larger goats went with Billy, while the mothers and young Nannies stayed behind.

"Where are the kids?" called out Daisy. "They were here just a minute ago."

"I guess they have gone with their father and grandfather," replied Nannie.

"I shall have to go after them then for they are sure to get into trouble, and besides I want them with me if anything happens."

"Yes, bring them back, and I will look after one and not let him out of my sight a moment, while you look out for the other."

"You stay here," commanded Stubby, who had not yet joined the crowd by the fence. "I'll bring them both back."

And presently they saw Stubby driving the two kids in front of him. If they tried to turn back, he snapped at their heels, and if they tried to separate, he grabbed them by the neck and made them march straight to where their mother and grandmother were waiting.

The Twins were crying and pleading to go back. "Uncle Stubby, do let us go back! We want to see the escaped panther! We never saw one!" they said.

"Escaped panther, did I hear them say?" Daisy asked Stubby.

"Yes. One of the largest panthers has escaped. When his keeper opened the cage door to put in a bucket of water, he opened the door a little wider than usual, and the panther that was lying on a ledge in the upper part of the cage leaped for the opening, hit the door which threw it still wider and he escaped. The keeper had enough presence of mind to slam the door shut as the mate awoke from a nap and also made for the door. When she found herself shut in and her mate gone, she made such a row she has upset all the animals. Anything like this always excites the animals and makes them roar and slash around in their cages trying to break through to freedom too.

"And now I want to tell you to be most watchful. For panthers are fond of goats and sheep—they like them best of all meats. They may smell goats and come over here to eat a kid or two," and Stubby looked straight at the kids, his face very sober, trying to frighten them so they would keep close to their mother and not run away again.

By this time men were running all over the Park with loaded pistols and guns in their hands, while others carried pitchforks and ropes to try to lasso the panther for they really wished to capture him alive if they could.

Mothers with children hurried out of the Park, and soon few people could be seen except the Park guards and the men who were hunting the loose beast. It was about four o'clock when the escape was made and at dusk they had not found him yet. The animals quieted down when they were given their supper, forgetting that one of their number had gained the much-desired freedom. All but the panther's mate. She refused to be comforted, but snarled and showed her teeth when any one went near her cage.

It was just that hour between twilight and darkness when shapes can still be distinguished moving about that Billy chanced to look up in the big tree that stood near the fence of the goat yard. He thought he saw two yellow balls of fire about the size of big marbles shining up among the leaves in the tree. As he looked, they seemed to move slowly toward him. Then looking more closely, he made out the outline of a big panther crouching on the limb ready to spring down on the unsuspecting Angoras peacefully sleeping directly under the limb the beast was on.

Billy gave the alarm, but too late. The panther had made a spring and landed on the back of a young Angora goat and was now devouring it greedily, while all the rest of the goats ran over to where Billy and his family stood in an opposite corner of the yard.

"All of you big goats with horns get ready to fight," commanded Billy, "for the minute that panther has devoured that victim, he will come over here for another nice young, juicy goat."

"Oh, my darlings! He will pick them out," wailed Daisy, "because they are the very youngest and will make the most tender eating."

"Don't cry, Daisy. He hasn't gotten them yet, and he won't while I am alive," said Billy Whiskers.

"Nor while I breathe either!" exclaimed Billy Junior, not to be outdone.

When the panther had finished his meal, he stood up, looked around, licked his chops, switched his tail, and called for his mate to come and join him in the feast. But that call was his undoing. His mate could not get out of her cage, but the panther's keeper recognized his voice and hastily calling some men and guards, he started to find the panther by going in the direction of the call. As the moon had come up in full glory, they had no trouble in locating him.

They found him none too soon, for just as they appeared at the fence, the panther started toward the goats to select another victim. He had his eye on one of the Twins, that Billy Whiskers could see. Brave as could be, Billy walked out of the herd and straight at the panther, intending to try to drive him away at least, but he knew it would be almost impossible as these beasts are strong, as quick as a cat and are bloodthirsty fighters.

When Billy Junior saw his father advancing on the panther, he too left the herd and walked out by Billy. Then Stubby and Button followed. This in no way frightened the panther. He still advanced on them, crouching as he came and ready to spring at any moment.

Billy Senior whispered, "We must make a rush at him or he will spring over our heads and we can't reach him. When I say three, spring at him prepared to rip him open with your horns. I will do the same. We can't both miss him. And, Stubby, you go for his neck, and, Button, you try to scratch his eyes out, so he can't see where to jump. One, two—"

But what had happened? The panther was jerked back off his feet and lay sprawling on his back, his feet in the air. This is what had occurred:

The men had come up to the yard behind the panther and goats so none of the animals had seen them. The man with the lasso had climbed the fence and thrown it, catching the panther around the neck just as he was about to spring, while the other men stood with pistols aimed and ready to fire did the lasso fail to go around the panther's neck and pull him back in time to save the goats.

"Gee! Those two goats and that dog and cat had nerve to face that beast," said one of the men. "I should like to own them for pets."

"So should I," replied one of the others. "Let us get that panther out of their yard and then give the goats a rousing good supper to show we admire bravery in animals as well as in people."

So it happened that the men all came back carrying bunches of clover and other things they thought the goats would like to eat.

When they dragged the panther out they closed the gate, but neglected to close it tightly. They had no sooner gotten out of sight than Billy said, "Now is our chance for freedom. The gate can easily be pushed open far enough for us to squeeze through."

He told the Angora goats about it, but they had been in captivity so long they did not yearn for freedom, as they had no homes to go to. Besides, they were well treated where they were and so they decided to go out into the Park and roam around a little, but not to run away.

"Well, we are all going to make our escape and skedaddle for home. So good-by to you all!"

"Here is wishing you and your family a safe and happy journey," bleated the leader of the Angora flock.

"The same to you and yours!" baaed Billy as he, his family and friends filed out the gate and started on a run toward their old home in Fon du Lac, Wisconsin.

THE END